D0349833

PLAYLIST
FOR THE
DEAD

An Imprint of HarperCollinsPublishers

HarperTeen is an imprint of HarperCollins Publishers.

Playlist for the Dead
 For information address HarperCollins Children's Books, a division of HarperCollins Publishers, 195 Broadway, New York, NY 10007.
www.epicreads.com

Library of Congress Cataloging-in-Publication Data
Falkoff, Michelle.
Playlist for the dead / Michelle Falkoff. — First edition.
pages cm
Summary: After his best friend, Hayden, commits suicide, fifteen-year-old Sam is determined to find out why—using the clues in the playlist Hayden left for him.
ISBN 978-0-06-231050-7
[1. Friendship—Fiction. 2. Loss (Psychology)—Fiction. 3. Suicide—Fiction. 4. Coming of age—Fiction.] I. Title.
PZ7.1.F35Pl 2015 2014022035
[Fic]—dc23 CIP
AC

Typography by Ellice M. Lee
14 15 16 17 18 CG/RRDH 10 9 8 7 6 5 4 3 2 1
❖
First Edition

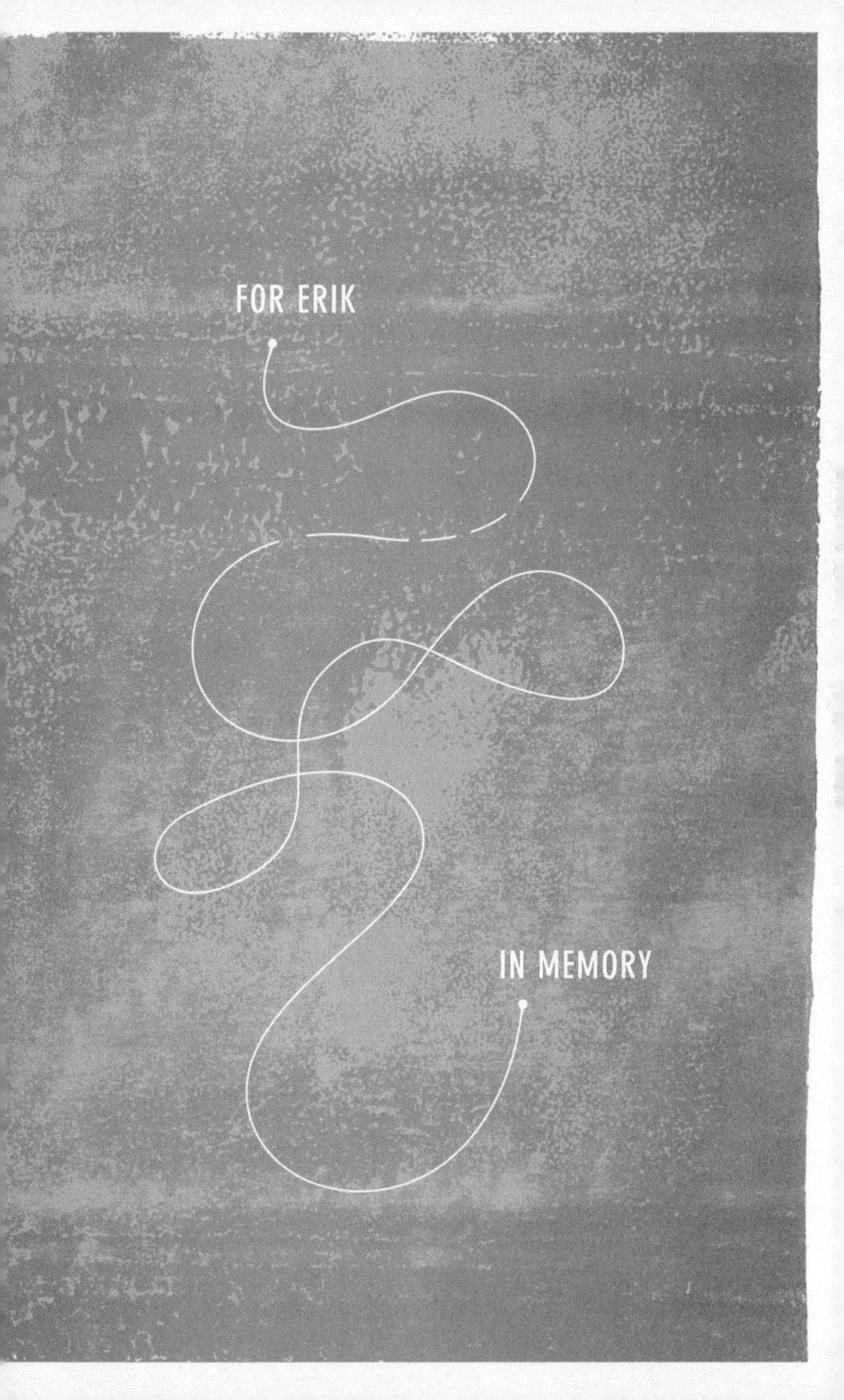
FOR ERIK
IN MEMORY

ALL MY YEARS of watching TV made me think it was possible you could find a dead body and not know it until you turned the person over and found the bullet hole or stab wound or whatever. And I guess in some ways that was right—Hayden was lying under the covers, tangled up in a bunch of his lame-ass Star Wars sheets (how old were we, anyway?), just like he always was when I slept at his house.

Hayden had always been a hard sleeper; sometimes I had to practically roll him out of bed to get him to wake up. Which wasn't easy—he was short and kind of round, and while I'm a lot taller, I'm more of a string bean kind of guy, and when he was out cold he was hard to move. When I saw him lying there I sighed, trying to figure out how to incorporate the apology from the night before, the apology I'd come over to give him, with the apology for dumping him out of bed onto the floor.

The sound of my sigh seemed loud to me, though, and it took me a minute to figure out why: Hayden wasn't snoring. Hayden always snored. My mom, who's a nurse, thought he had sleep apnea; the sound of his buzzing made it all the way down the hall to her room when he stayed at my house. She kept trying to get him to talk to his mom about getting some kind of mask that would help, but I knew that would never happen. Hayden didn't talk to his mom unless he absolutely had to, and he was even less likely to ask his dad.

The silence in the room started to freak me out. I kept trying to convince myself it was nothing, that Hayden had just found a good position to sleep in that quieted his steady drone or something, but that would have been some kind of minor miracle, and even after five years of Hebrew school I didn't really believe in miracles.

I gave his leg a little shove. "Hayden, come on."

He didn't move.

"Hayden, seriously. Wake up."

Nothing. Not even a grunt.

I was just about to grab a stormtrooper's head and pull down the sheets when I saw the empty vodka bottle on Hayden's desk, standing in between his laptop and his model of the *Millennium Falcon*, just next to where he was sleeping.

That was weird—Hayden didn't drink at all, not even at the few parties we'd been to. And from what I could tell he hadn't had time to take as much as a sip from the keg last night. There was no reason for that bottle to be there. Unless he'd been even more bent out of shape than I realized; he could easily have taken it out of his dad's liquor cabinet when he got home.

I felt my stomach churn with what I realized was guilt. That must have been why he wouldn't wake up: he was hung over. Even through my guilt, I couldn't help but start laughing. Hayden's first hangover—I was going to give him so much shit for this when he finally woke up. Then I'd drag him off for a greasy breakfast and we'd make up. And everything would be fine.

Now he just had to wake up.

I moved closer to the head of the bed, sniffing cautiously in case he'd puked. The air smelled like it normally did in his house: overly disinfected, the pine scent overwhelming anything else. I swear his mom must have had cleaners come in every single day. I debated whether to roll him over or just pull the pillow out from beneath his head, but just as I went for the pillow I knocked over the empty vodka bottle with my elbow. It fell to the floor with a clang, taking down some other stuff with it.

I bent over to pick it up. No need to have Hayden wake up pissed that I'd made a mess; we had enough to talk about as it was. I grabbed the bottle, and then I saw a prescription bottle next to it and grabbed that too. It was a bottle of Valium with Hayden's mother's name on it. And it was empty.

I didn't know how many pills were supposed to have been in there, but according to the date on the bottle, she'd filled the prescription just a couple of days before. Which meant she'd gone through a whole bottle practically overnight.

I looked at the vodka bottle.

Or Hayden had.

And then I saw one more thing I'd knocked on the floor. A thumb drive, next to a torn-off scrap of notebook paper. *For Sam*, it read. *Listen and you'll understand.*

That's when I called 911.

1

"HOW TO DISAPPEAR COMPLETELY"

RADIOHEAD

THE MORNING OF HAYDEN'S FUNERAL I couldn't get out of bed. I don't mean that I didn't want to—if anything, I wanted the day to go by as quickly as possible, and if getting up was the first step, then I was in.

But I couldn't do it.

It was a weird feeling, kind of like being stuck in a block of ice. I pictured that scene from *Star Wars* where Han Solo gets frozen in carbonite, hands in front of him as if he could somehow protect himself, mouth half open in silent protest. It was an image Hayden had always found haunting; he said it freaked him out every time he saw it, and he'd seen *The Empire Strikes Back* maybe a thousand times. I'd seen it nearly as many but for some reason I thought the whole carbonite thing was hilarious, and it was even funnier how twitchy it made Hayden. For his birthday I'd bought him an iPhone cover with the frozen Han Solo image on it, and I'd slipped frozen Han Solo ice cubes into his soda.

Remembering the look on his face made me laugh, and laughing seemed to break the spell. I could move again, though I didn't want to anymore. Moving meant I was awake, and being awake meant Hayden was really dead, and I wasn't quite ready to admit that yet. And laughing felt wrong, but also good, and the fact that it made me feel good also made me feel guilty, which brought me back to wrong. Really, I didn't know how to feel. Sad? Check. Pissed off? Definitely.

What were you thinking, Hayden?

"What?" My mother cracked the door open and peered in at me. Her curly brown hair was twisted into a braid, and she was wearing a dress instead of scrubs. "Did you ask me something, Sam?"

"No, just talking to myself." I hadn't realized I'd said it out loud.

She opened the door wider. "Still in bed? Come on, we've got to get cracking here. You know I'm not going to be able to stay for the whole thing—I'm going to be late for work as it is." She snapped her fingers a couple of times. She wasn't exactly the warm and fuzzy type.

"I can't get ready if you don't get out." It came out sharper than I meant it to, but she must have understood because she closed the door without saying anything, but not before hanging something on the back of my door on her way out. A suit, the one I'd worn to my cousin's wedding last summer.

She must have ironed it for me. I felt like even more of a jerk than I already did.

I got out of bed, turned on my computer, and pulled up the playlist I'd found on Hayden's thumb drive. He'd left it for me, knowing I would find it, probably even knowing I'd find him—I was always the one to apologize first after our fights. I couldn't stand staying mad. He must have realized I'd come over, even after how we'd left things.

I'd been listening to it constantly over the past couple of days, trying to figure out what he meant. *Listen and you'll understand.* What was I supposed to understand? He'd killed himself and left me here all alone, left me to find him. And I was pretty sure it was my fault, though that wasn't something I was prepared to think about at the moment. But I'd listened and listened, looking for the song that would confirm it, the song that would lay all the blame on me. So far I hadn't found it.

Instead, I'd found a confusing collection of music from all over the spectrum—some recent stuff, some older. Some songs I knew; others I didn't, and given that Hayden and I had developed our taste together—or so I thought—that was surprising. I'd have to keep listening to see if I could figure out what he'd been talking about, though I wasn't sure what the point was.

I scanned the list for something funeral-appropriate. Most of the songs were pretty depressing, so there wasn't an obvious choice; I started with a song that reminded me of the first time I'd worn the suit I was about to put on. It was gray and a little shiny and I'd worn it with a bow tie. My cousins, preppie throwbacks, already thought I was weird, so why not give them some proof? Mom was cool about it, just said she was happy I had a sense of personal style and an opinion about my clothes. She'd been a sharp dresser herself, back when she and my dad were still together, when she used to try. Now she rarely changed out of the scrubs she wore to work. Rachel, my older sister, was less cool about the suit and called me a dork in a bunch of different ways before Mom made her go back upstairs and change out of the dress she'd wanted to wear. Which, let's be honest, was kind of trashy for a family wedding.

Hayden had come over as I was getting ready, to see if I wanted to go to the mall with him. And by "mall," he basically meant one store—the only store we ever went to. The Intergalactic Trading Company. The rest of the kids at school tended to hang out on the other end, near the sporting goods store. We rarely went down there. I'd forgotten to tell him about the wedding.

"Nice suit," he said, in his quiet way, making it hard for me to tell if he was being serious or sarcastic. I was never sure, with Hayden. With me it was easy; I was always being a wiseass.

"Whatever. You wouldn't be caught dead in one, right?" I

winced now, remembering it, but even then I knew it wasn't really true. Hayden would do whatever his parents told him. He didn't like it, but it was better than the alternative.

He shrugged. "The bow tie helps," he said. "But it would look way cooler with a T-shirt under it. Like this one." He picked up the Radiohead shirt lying at the foot of my bed, the one he'd given me after going to see them on tour. It read HOW IT ENDS, HOW IT STARTS.

I rolled my eyes. "Does it really have to be Radiohead?"

"What's wrong with Radiohead?" he asked, but he knew what I was going to say. We'd had this argument a million times.

"Some of their stuff is okay," I said. "But what really makes them different from Coldplay? White English dudes who went to fancy universities and are probably too smart for their own good. But girls think Chris Martin is hot, and they think Thom Yorke is weird-looking, and so Coldplay sells a bazillion albums and Radiohead has to reach out to geeks like us. Something about it just doesn't seem right."

"You're way off," he said. "Radiohead is on a different planet than Coldplay. *Kid A* might be the greatest record ever made, and Coldplay gets sued for plagiarism every time they release a single. Just talking about them at the same time is, like, disrespectful to Radiohead."

I loved getting Hayden all riled up. Back when we were little, Mom would worry about how much we fought. She'd come into my room when we were yelling at each other—okay, I was yelling; Hayden was rationally and patiently trying to explain his position, even as a kid—and she'd knock on the door. "Everything okay in there?"

"We're fine," we'd both say. And we were.

Just remembering it made me miss him.

I stopped getting ready for a minute and focused on the music coming out of my speakers. I wasn't surprised he'd put "How to Disappear Completely" on his mix, since it was his favorite song ("Idioteque" was mine—despite how I needled Hayden, I agreed that Radiohead was infinitely better than Coldplay). I tried not to think too hard about the lyrics, about Hayden sitting there putting together this mix before making his final decision. I hated imagining him wanting to fade away like that.

My fists clenched, fingernails digging into my palms, and I tried to calm down. I'd spent the past few days alternating between missing him and hating him, feeling guilty and shitty, not knowing how I was supposed to be feeling but wanting it to be different, somehow. He'd left me alone, and I'd never have done that to him, no matter how mad I was. It had made it almost impossible to sleep, so on top of everything else I was exhausted. Exhausted and angry. A great combination.

Except being mad just started the cycle again, a cycle that was becoming familiar. Get angry. Blame Hayden. Feel guilty. Miss him. Get angry again. This was punctuated occasionally with the urge to scream or hit things, neither of which I could manage to do. Why couldn't I be normal and just feel sad, like other people?

"Sam, get a move on!" Mom called from downstairs.

Back to missing him. I needed to do something to make myself feel better, though. I went to the laundry basket, dug out my old Radiohead T-shirt, and put it on under the suit.

2

"CROWN OF LOVE"

ARCADE FIRE

THE CHURCH WHERE THE FUNERAL was being held was on the east side of Libertyville, the rich side. The Stevenses, Hayden's family, lived there. Mine didn't.

From the outside the church looked almost like a really fancy ski lodge, all dark wood and exposed beams—it had probably been built by one of the architects responsible for all the McMansions on that side of town. The wood was lighter on the inside, which had a high arched ceiling and a sparkly modern-looking chandelier hanging down. Almost like they wanted people to forget it was a church.

My family was Jewish, so the only church I'd ever been to was the Catholic one on my side of town, where all the kids I went to school with had their First Communions. We'd just moved to town so I didn't really know anyone, but one of the kids in my class had invited everyone to his and Mom said I had to go if I wanted to make friends, though it didn't really work out like that.

The Catholic church had looked more like what I'd expect a church to look like: white on the outside, with a crucifix at the altar and lots of stained-glass windows. This church looked almost nothing like it, except for the fact that there were two columns of pews that ended with an altar. At the foot of that altar was a coffin, and in that coffin was Hayden. Probably also wearing a suit.

By the time we showed up the place was almost full. Rachel had taken off to sit with her friends as soon as we walked in the door, shocker, and so it was just me and Mom walking up and down the aisles, trying to find seats. The first few rows were filled with Hayden's family—I saw his parents and Ryan, his older brother, as well as some aunts and uncles and cousins I recognized from the times I'd gone to Hayden's house over the holidays. Since my family didn't celebrate Christmas, Hayden would invite me over to have dessert with them after they'd finished opening their presents and having their big fancy dinner. Hayden was always grateful if I showed up, since it got him away from the table faster. His mom was always on his case about how much he ate, and Christmas was the worst. If he even looked at a second piece of pie, she'd give him a sharp look and say, "Do you really need that, Hayden?" But Hayden would never fight back. He wasn't like that. He'd do anything to keep the peace.

They'd never deserved him, his family.

The rows behind Hayden's family were filled with obnoxious rich people from his side of town and their obnoxious kids, friends of Ryan's who'd spent years torturing Hayden, some at Ryan's direction. They all thought life would always be as easy for them as it was right now. Rich jocks like Jason Yoder who hired tutors to get them through the hard classes; girls like Stephanie Caster with nose jobs and personal trainers who would have been beautiful without either but who now all looked exactly alike. I mean, they were still cute, don't get me wrong, but it wasn't the same. It made me furious, seeing them all sitting there, acting like they were so sad when all of this was at least partly their fault. How could I feel so out of place at my own best friend's funeral?

Mom put her hand on my shoulder. The weight of it was comforting; I was glad I didn't have to be here alone. "We've got to sit somewhere, sweetie." She steered me toward the back of the room, into one of the pews near the church door. "I know you want to sit closer, but they're going to start soon and there just isn't room."

I nodded, reminding myself to unclench my fists.

"You'll need to check in with Rachel—she's going to arrange for you guys to get a ride home, okay? I'm so sorry," she said.

"Sure." It wasn't surprising, but I wasn't upset by it—Mom was always having to take off early, or come home late. When Dad left for good she'd gone back to school nights to become a nurse practitioner, and since the hospital was understaffed she'd signed up for as much overtime as she could get, especially since Dad was kind of a slacker about sending checks. We weren't in bad shape, she told Rachel and me, but we weren't working with a whole lot of cushion, either. Not like the people sitting at the front of the church.

I struggled to get comfortable on the wooden bench as everyone began to settle down. It was already fifteen minutes after the service was supposed to start, and I could still hear people coming in behind me. For a guy with basically one friend, his funeral was pretty crowded.

He'd have hated it, I was sure. He'd have been sitting here in the back, with me.

I felt hot and itchy. I was starting to sweat under my shiny suit. I thought about leaving, but I was trapped in the row—Mom had snagged the seat on the end so she could duck out quietly, and some random woman in a brightly flower-printed dress had me pinned on the other side. Weren't people supposed to wear black to funerals? She looked like she was off to a fucking garden party.

I felt the urge to hit something again and tried to find a way to focus so I could calm down. I listened to the music that was being piped through the speaker system. No organ here. I didn't recognize the song; it was some kind of New Age elevator music, all soothing, with flutes. Another thing that would have made Hayden nuts. I wondered whether he'd picked one of the songs on the playlist especially for his funeral, and I tried to figure out which one it might be. The best I could come up with was an old Arcade Fire song from their *Funeral* album. We both loved Arcade Fire. We actually watched the Grammys when they won Album of the Year, the first time either of us had had any interest in that show since we were little kids.

After another ten minutes the minister stood up at the altar. He began to drone on about the tragedy of losing someone so young, all platitudes and euphemisms and none of the words that described what had really happened. It made me so crazy I just stared straight ahead at the backs of people's heads. A few rows in front of me, a girl with long white-blond hair with black streaks in it leaned on the shoulder of some tall hipster dude. I didn't recognize either one of them, at least not from the back. I couldn't help but think it was funny that her hair seemed funeral-appropriate, compared with the woman in the garden-party dress.

When the actual prayers started Mom kissed the top of my head and said, "Gotta go," leaving as quietly as her nursing clogs would let her. I felt bad she had to work so many hours on her feet that she'd soak them when she got home, most nights. I'd offered to get an after-school job once I'd turned fifteen, a few months ago, but she just laughed. "Long gone are the days that teenagers could get jobs at the mall," she said. "Half the moms I know at the PTA are working at the Gap. You don't have a shot, kiddo. Just keep studying and I'll hit you up for some help when I retire."

She was joking, but only sort of. I knew there were kids at school whose moms were waiting tables at Olive Garden, or selling makeup and jewelry from their east-side basements, pretending it was just for fun, as if they didn't need to start helping out if they wanted to keep living there. Ever since the Liberty Appliance Factory closed, a few years ago, the line between the rich people and the people who were struggling to get by had gotten blurry. It was nice of Mom to at least go in late; I tried to remember not to be mad at her for leaving me here.

After the prayers, the minister started asking for testimonials. "Anyone who wants to speak, anyone who has something to share," he said. There was an awkward pause. Finally, Hayden's father stood up. I couldn't bear to look at him, to see him crying as if he'd lost something so valuable to him, when I knew the truth, how he spent all his time at work or traveling or visiting the woman Hayden knew he was sleeping with, the one who went on all his business trips with him.

But I couldn't block out the sound of his voice. "Hayden wasn't the son I expected to have," he said. "I'd imagined playing catch in the yard, watching football on the weekends, going fishing. The things I'd done with my dad; the things I do with Ryan. It was the only kind of relationship I knew how to have with a son." His voice cracked. "But my second son didn't enjoy any of those things. He loved music and video games and computers. I didn't know how to talk to him. And now I'll spend the rest of my life wishing I'd learned how." He lowered his head, as if he were trying to hide the fact that he was crying.

It was a great performance. If only a single word of it were true.

I looked over to see Ryan in the front row. He was shaking his head, which surprised me. I would have thought he'd agree with every word that came out of his father's mouth, like he always did.

I thought about getting up there, what I could say about my best friend, the stories I could tell. I could talk about how we'd met at a Little League tryout when we were eight, not that long after I'd moved to Libertyville. Neither of us had wanted to be there; Hayden was short and chubby even then, and to say I was uncoordinated was a pretty serious understatement. We both missed every pitch, dropped every ball thrown to us from even the shortest distance, and finally we'd run away from the field, pooling our change to buy one of those orange Dreamsicle pops from the ice-cream truck. Our parents had been furious, but we didn't care.

I could talk about waiting in line to get into *Phantom Menace 3-D* when we were twelve, not realizing how crappy it was going to be, how we'd spent months trying to decide what costumes we'd wear, ditching the obvious—C-3PO for me, R2-D2 for him—in exchange for Boba Fett and Darth Vader, because they were more badass. I could talk about how Ryan and his buddies had followed us and egged our costumes and we'd had to sit through the endless movie feeling the eggs drying on our costumes and our skin, but we'd still had a good time.

I could talk about how excited we'd been to start high school last year, the first time we'd be at the same school, how convinced we'd been that once we were together things would be better. We couldn't have known how wrong that would turn out to be.

But what would be the point of saying any of those things? Everyone might pretend to care now, but it was too late.

And then I saw the line. People were getting up to speak, standing in a row to the side of the altar. Hayden's aunts and cousins, teachers, friends of the family. Kids from school. Ryan, on his own, without his usual buddies, Jason Yoder and Trevor Floyd. We'd called them the bully trifecta.

It shouldn't have been shocking to me, to see who'd decided they had something to say at Hayden's funeral. They were all starved for attention, and there wasn't a chance they'd miss the opportunity to grab the spotlight, no matter what the occasion. But seriously, at a funeral? Were they really going to get up there and say nice things about Hayden, talk about how much they'd miss him, what a loss it would be for the school, the community? Did they have no sense of how much they'd contributed to the fact that we were all here in the first place?

There was no way I could let this happen. All the anger I'd been feeling, the urge to find someone responsible and hit them as hard as I could, boiled in me. I walked up to Ryan and tapped him on the shoulder while one of Hayden's cousins was tearfully recounting some story about Thanksgiving, the last time the whole family had been together. Ryan frowned when he saw it was me. I was just about to say something when Jason Yoder stepped in between us. I hadn't realized he was so close.

"You really think now's the time?" he asked.

I moved to the right to get around him, only to be blocked again by Trevor Floyd.

"Let me by," I said. I wasn't scared of them. Not now.

"I don't think so," Jason said.

He was the only one of the three who wasn't an athlete, and I was taller than he was. I pushed him aside to get to Ryan. It wasn't like Trevor was going to deck me at a funeral.

"What are you doing?" I asked. "You're really going to get up there and talk about what a great brother you were? When everyone here knows the truth? You were at that party just like me. You could have stopped things. You should have protected him, not made everything worse."

Ryan opened his mouth, but before he could get the words

out Jason shoved me so hard I banged into one of the pews. I saw people looking at us even as I tried—and failed—to keep from falling down.

"You're really going to go after Ryan at his brother's funeral?" Jason hissed. I'd underestimated his strength; I'd been more worried about the enormous Trevor, who was six and a half feet tall with the thick neck I'd learned was common to steroid users—kids at school called him Roid Floyd, but only behind his back. He wasn't someone I was looking to get into a fight with. Especially not here.

I stood up as carefully as I could. My arms would be covered in bruises tomorrow, but I wasn't about to let the bully trifecta see me fall down. "You're a fucking hypocrite," I said to Ryan. "And someday you'll get what's coming to you."

Ryan didn't say anything, just stared at me for a minute. Then he moved forward in line. It was almost his turn to speak.

I couldn't watch this. I couldn't wait for Rachel to find us a ride. I had to leave. Now.

3

"MAD WORLD"

TEARS FOR FEARS/GARY JULES

THE MALL WAS MAYBE TWO MILES away from the church, right near the border between the east and west sides of town. It was the middle of October and the weather hadn't turned that cold yet, but it was pretty dank. The sky was a flatter gray than my suit, which matched my mood. Still, walking felt good, so I didn't hurry; I just put in my earbuds and listened to Hayden's playlist as I walked. I stuck mostly to the main drag, Burlington Street, past the downtown coffeehouses and restaurants, past the run-down museum of local history that marked the unofficial transition to the west side of town. The Libertyville Mall was just beyond the museum, but it was a combination of upscale and downmarket, as the real-estate people would say, just like the town itself. The anchor stores on one end were Nordstrom and Dillard's; on the other end were JCPenney and Sears. Near the fancy end were boutiques and jewelry stores; the other end had the

Payless shoe store and cheap clothing chains. The rich people were always fighting to close down the trashier stores so they could open a Whole Foods and a Trader Joe's, but nothing ever happened. Typical.

It took me about an hour to get to the entrance, but I knew immediately where I wanted to go. The Intergalactic Trading Company was near the front door at the Sears end, its windows darkened and glowing with purple light. It had once been one of those gift stores that sold weird novelty items and lava lamps, and I guess they'd kept some of the décor. But the ITC was way too awesome to be all about whoopee cushions and fake barf. It was basically sci-fi/fantasy/geek heaven—it sold vintage Star Wars action figures, Magic: The Gathering playing cards, Mage Warfare figurines, Star Trek posters, comic books, and video games. Just about anything I could ever want.

I wandered the aisles, remembering all the conversations Hayden and I had had during the many hours we'd spent here. We'd ranked the Star Trek TV series (I insisted *Next Generation* was first, while Hayden was adamant that the old series was the best). We'd tried to start a Dungeons & Dragons club when we didn't make the Little League team, but we couldn't get anyone else to see the beauty of the twenty-sided die. We'd get there first thing in the morning when the new *Walking Dead* comic came out every month and would sit in the food court reading it from cover to cover. We loved the TV show too, and watched it at my house every Sunday night. It was the only time Rachel deigned to hang out with us.

It was really hard to be here without him.

The store was all but deserted in the middle of the day. After school there was usually a bunch of kids wandering around, geeks like Hayden and me, and younger kids, too. When we'd come at night there were often older guys there, collectors, I figured, with day jobs. But this was a place the assholes from school never came. It was a safe place. True, there were almost never any girls here, but guys like me and Hayden didn't tend to do so well with the ladies anyway.

Maybe I'd spoken too soon, because as I walked around, I noticed a couple of other people browsing, and one of them was a girl. Definitely a girl. Tall, like me, with kind of a pointy face—sharp chin, straight skinny nose. Her mouth was painted a deep burgundy and she had a lip ring with a turquoise stud in it. And a big mass of whitish-blond hair, with black streaks. She was the girl from the funeral. She was cute. Well, more interesting-looking than cute, but whatever look she was going for, I was into it.

And she seemed to be headed right for me.

I felt a rising sense of panic and fought the urge to hide.

Then she was right in front of me, and her mouth was moving but I couldn't understand anything she was saying. What was wrong with me?

I must have looked really confused, because she smiled,

reached out her hand, and pulled on the wire dangling in front of me.

Of course—I still had my earbuds in. No wonder I couldn't hear her; I'd been blaring music from the playlist.

"You're Sam, aren't you?" she repeated.

She knew me? How did she know me? I nodded.

"Is that all you've got?" she asked. "Usually when someone initiates an introduction, you should ask her name."

"Sorry," I said. Figures I'd screw up my first conversation with a girl who actually seemed willing to talk to me. Still, I couldn't tell if she was being serious. "I guess I'm a little out of it today." She had to understand, right? She'd been at the funeral too.

"Understandable," she said, and kind of smirked at me. So she had been kidding? I still wasn't sure. "I'm Astrid."

"Cool name."

She smiled widely. "Picked it out myself."

Before I could ask her anything else, the lanky hipster-looking dude from the funeral walked up in his super-tight skinny pants and put his arm around her. She turned to him and leaned her head on his shoulder, like I'd seen her do before. "And this is Eric. Eric, this is Sam. Hayden's friend."

Did that mean she knew Hayden? She couldn't have—I'd know. But she knew who I was, and that didn't make sense either. I didn't think anyone knew who I was.

"Sorry to hear about your friend," Eric said. "He sounded

like a good guy, from what Astrid's told me."

So she did know Hayden. I couldn't imagine how. And why wouldn't he have told me? "He was," I said.

"Anyway, didn't mean to interrupt. I'll just be outside, whenever you're ready." He flicked Astrid in the arm and left the store. It seemed like a weird gesture for someone I assumed was probably her boyfriend, but I was hardly an expert on romantic relationships.

I was dying to know how Astrid knew Hayden, but I didn't know where to start.

Luckily, I didn't have to. "Look, I swear I'm not some crazy stalker, and I didn't mean to freak you out, but I did follow you here," Astrid said. "I just wanted a chance to tell you how sorry I am about Hayden. I only knew him for a little while, but he was a really nice guy, and I still can't believe he's really gone."

"Me neither," I said. "So . . . you guys knew each other?"

"Sort of," she said, and pulled on one of the black streaks in her hair. "I know you guys were friends, and I saw you leave when all those hypocrites got in line to make speeches about him, so I thought you might like to know that there are other people out there who are going to miss him. For real."

I knew she'd said "were" because Hayden was gone, not because he and I weren't friends anymore. Still, I couldn't help thinking about the night he died and how awful everything had been, especially between us. I didn't want to look at Astrid—I didn't want her to see whatever look was on my face and think it was because of her—so I turned to the glass case next to where we were standing, which held action figures from various games and other trinkets.

"Hayden used to make fun of people who bought stuff like this," I said. "He called them dolls for dorks, as if that was going to somehow distinguish us from them."

"Kind of like that Venn diagram of dorks versus geeks versus nerds?" she asked.

"You've seen that too?" I asked. Was this some kind of joke? A girl follows me into my favorite store and knows all about the stuff I'm into? "Anyway, one of these figurines kind of reminds me of Hayden's character in Mage Warfare." I waited for her to ask me what that was, but she didn't. This was getting even stranger, but in a kind of awesome way. I'd never met a girl who knew what Mage Warfare was. But then again, I'd hardly hung out with any girls.

"Which one?"

I pointed to one of the figurines. It was maybe four inches tall, a long-haired man in a cloak and a floppy hat, holding a wand.

"A wizard?" she asked.

"It's actually more of a warlock, or a magus. A disciple of Zoroaster, the inventor of magic." I paused when I thought I saw her eyes glaze over. Apparently I could still be too dorky, even with a girl who seemed to get it. "I mean, yeah, wizard works."

"Aren't you just full of useful information?" she said, with another smirk. "Doesn't look much like Hayden, though."

It was true; Hayden hadn't really hit his growth spurt yet, and his mother's nagging him to eat more protein and skip dessert had only made him stubborn. Physically the magus looked more like me, tall and skinny, not unlike Astrid's hipster boyfriend. But the whole point of living in a fantasy world was the fantasy, right? My character was a golem, strong and sturdy like I wasn't and probably would never be, unless I turned into one of those gym rats and started lifting weights all the time. I'd probably drop them on myself anyway. "It's a role-playing game," I said. "He could be whoever he wanted there."

"Sounds liberating," she said. "I think you should buy it if it reminds you of him. A keepsake."

"So I won't forget him?" I tried not to sound bitter.

Either she didn't hear the sour note in my voice or it didn't bother her. "You'll never forget him. But you're not going to make it through the rest of the school year, or the rest of high school, if you think about him all the time. If you have this, you'll have a place to focus. You can think about him when you look at it, and the rest of the time you can try to live."

"Sounds like you know what you're talking about."

"I've been through some stuff," she said. Cryptic, like

Hayden was. I could see why they might have been friends. "Trust me on this one."

"I will," I said. "Thanks."

"No problem." She reached over again and picked up one of the earbuds dangling from my neck. I hoped she couldn't feel my pulse starting to speed up. "What were you listening to, when I so rudely interrupted you?"

"It wasn't rude," I said, but she'd already stuck the earbud in her ear.

"Come on, press play," she said.

I put the other earbud in my ear, hit the button, and listened with her. It was a song from the playlist, haunting and beautiful. Listening to it with her felt otherworldly, like we'd somehow left the store and wandered off by ourselves, into some dark and creepy forest. But together. I closed my eyes and kept listening.

"Gary Jules," she said, and I snapped out of it, opening my eyes to the fluorescent lighting. Astrid was looking right at me; I hoped she didn't think it was weird that I'd closed my eyes. "From the *Donnie Darko* soundtrack. It's a cover of an old Tears for Fears song."

I knew the original version, but I hadn't heard the cover until the playlist. It didn't sound like something Hayden would normally listen to, and I wondered about the fact that Astrid had immediately recognized it. "You've seen the movie?" I asked.

"A bunch of times. It's amazing. You should totally watch it and tell me what you think."

"Will do," I said, and I knew it was true. I wanted to ask her more questions, to find out how she knew Hayden, to start, but out of the corner of my eye I could see Eric walking back into the store. *No*, I wanted to say. *Not yet.*

"Looks like it's time for me to go," Astrid said.

I wasn't about to ask her to stay in front of her boyfriend. I really wished she'd come alone, but then again, I might have made even more of an ass out of myself.

Astrid smoothed the collar on my suit, a gesture that would have felt motherly from someone older but which didn't feel motherly at all coming from her. Almost like we knew each other well enough that she had the right. I liked it. "Don't worry about all those people at the funeral. The ones who deserve it will get theirs someday. Karma, you know."

She sounded just like me. "Thanks."

"Find me at school," she said. "After you've watched the movie."

I could feel my arm tingling where her fingers had been even as she walked away, which highlighted how sore it already was from Jason knocking me into that pew. God, I hated those guys.

Once Astrid was gone, I went up to the counter and asked if I could see the magus figurine. The guy working there was the same guy who was there every time we came in.

Hayden and I had often wondered if the store had more than one employee. What would happen if he got sick? Or even just wanted a day off? He looked like one of the collectors: middle-aged and a little creepy. Maybe this was his dream job, and there was never anywhere else he wanted to be. I couldn't even imagine what kind of job that would be, for me.

"Where's your friend?" he asked. "I don't think I've ever seen you in here by yourself."

For some reason it hadn't occurred to me that there would be people who didn't know what had happened. And that I might have to explain it to them. I felt my face get hot as I started to panic at the idea of telling the store clerk about Hayden. I couldn't do it. "He's not here," I said. "Can I just look at the figurine, please?"

"No problem." He unlocked the glass case and handed the figurine to me. It felt heavy in my hands, cool to the touch, cast in pewter or some other metal and then painted. Not exactly expert craftsmanship—the paint was crudely applied and was already starting to chip.

I turned it over to see the price tag. "Thirty-five bucks for this?" I asked.

"It's a collectible," he said.

"Sure it is," I muttered.

"Look, do you want it or not?"

"Yeah," I said. "I do."

4

"INVISIBLE"

SKYLAR GREY

WHEN I GOT HOME FROM THE STORE I went straight to my room and unwrapped the magus figurine. What a stupid idea, buying something that would make me think of Hayden every time I looked at it. I hadn't stopped thinking about him since I found him; I couldn't get the image of him lying there not-asleep under those stupid Star Wars sheets out of my mind. The paramedics had made me leave the room as soon as they got there; I'd had to listen to them trying to revive him from the hallway, but I could hear everything they were saying. It had been way too late; he'd been dead for hours by the time I got there.

I thought about throwing the figurine out. So what if it meant blowing thirty-five dollars? Then I thought about throwing it out the window. Or through the window. The sound of glass shattering might be satisfying. But it was such a dinky little thing, and with my coordination it would probably bounce off the window without breaking so much as a pane of glass and hit me in the face.

Instead, I moved a stack of books from the shelf above my crappy old computer and set it there. I'd be able to see it when I played Mage Warfare, which seemed fitting. Maybe for a little while I could pretend that Hayden was playing with me, from his house, though this time we wouldn't interrupt our game to chat, like we usually did. Still, playing was the only thing I could imagine doing that would let me think about Hayden in a good way. I'd probably be better off taking a nap and trying to make up some of the hours of sleep I'd missed over the last week, but the walk had energized me a little and I figured I'd probably just lie in bed and go through the anger/guilt/missing-Hayden cycle over and over again.

No, playing the game would make me feel better. I put on Hayden's playlist, logged in to Mage Warfare, and clicked on my golem avatar. My mother had told me stories about mute monsters made out of clay who existed to protect old Jewish communities, and I'd read this amazing book about golems and comic books and all sorts of craziness. The golems in those stories had no power of their own and had to do whatever their creators told them to do. I'd kind of felt bad for them. I thought it might be fun to create one who had a mind of his own—okay, my mind—and who could take down anyone he wanted to with no repercussions. I had no interest in that kind of violence in real life; it was only fun for me here because it wasn't real. It was just a way to feel powerful somewhere, since I felt so powerless at school. My golem was named Brutus and he kicked ass on a regular basis.

Being in the game was like being in another world. I could almost pretend nothing had changed, that Hayden was still there, since we always played on opposite sides in Mage Warfare anyway. Hayden always had to be the good guy, fighting for the Cooperative, truth and justice and all that, while I liked playing for the bad guys. It was so different than who I was in real life, where I always worried about doing the right thing. What was so great about being a good guy, anyway? It's not like it ever got me anywhere. From what I could see, the worst jerks at school were the ones who all the teachers and other kids thought were so terrific—Ryan, Trevor, and Jason got all the girls, drove nice cars, had lots of money. Ryan made captain of the lacrosse team back when he was a junior; Trevor would probably skip college and go straight to the NHL; Jason was the best-looking guy in school and the treasurer of student council. They could do whatever they wanted, and no one seemed to care that they weren't such good people, that they had secrets. Whenever I got online I set up quests that pitted me against guys I figured were like them, players who wanted to be the center of attention, good at everything. And then I destroyed them.

Today I'd set myself up against a team of Alliance warriors. It was three on one, just like it had always been for

Hayden when Ryan and his buddies singled him out, but I was determined to kick some ass anyway. I was making such good progress I'd barely noticed how dark it had gotten until I heard the ping of my Gchat window. At first that seemed totally normal; I'd been playing for a while, and that was when Hayden would usually check in.

Except Hayden was dead, so it couldn't be Hayden.

I paused the game and looked away from the computer. It wasn't just darker than I thought; it was pitch black. I'd been playing longer than I realized. I rubbed my eyes and looked back at the computer.

Someone named Archmage_Ged was IMing me.

That made no sense. Archmage_Ged was Hayden's name in Mage Warfare—he'd based it on a character he loved from the *Wizard of Earthsea* books I'd loaned him as a kid, books he'd struggled to read. But he'd used his real name for Gchat.

I glanced up at the shelf where I'd put the wizard figurine, then looked back at the screen. Who would know to sign up for an account with that name? The glow of the computer monitor started to feel creepy, and the hairs on my arm were starting to stand on end.

The message said, *How do?*

I shivered, and all of a sudden I realized I was still alone in the house. Rachel hadn't come home, and Mom was still at work.

The cursor was blinking at me. *How do?*

That was how Hayden and I always started our Gchat conversations. We'd picked it up after spending a series of weekends powering through all five seasons of *The Wire.* But no one would know to start a conversation with me that way.

I looked at the computer screen again. It was still there. My job was usually to come up with something witty in response, but I just stared at the blinking cursor. There was no way it could be Hayden.

Archmage_Ged: You there?

Of course I was there; where else would I be? Hanging out with all my other friends? Oh, no, wait—I didn't have any.

Sam_Goldsmith: Who is this?
Archmage_Ged: Who do you think?

That was the thing—I couldn't think of who it could be. No one from school knew us well enough to imitate Hayden. Someone from Mage Warfare? We chatted inside the game all the time, so someone could have seen us use that name. But the chat request hadn't come from inside the game. This was my private email account. No one from the game had that info except Hayden.

Someone at school could have gotten it, though. Could it be one of the bully trifecta? Was this Ryan's way of getting back at me for yelling at him? As much as I disliked Ryan, though, I couldn't imagine him being evil enough to sneak away from his family the night of his brother's funeral just to screw with my head. Trevor was too stupid to pull off something like this, and from what Hayden had told me, Jason had his own stuff going on. It was possible; it just didn't seem all that likely. But I couldn't imagine who else it might be.

Sam_Goldsmith: Well, I know who it isn't.
Archmage_Ged: Are you sure?

Sure I was sure.

Sam_Goldsmith: Look, I don't know who you are or why you're doing this, but cut it out. Things are crappy enough as it is.
Archmage_Ged: Not messing with you. I'm here to help.
Sam_Goldsmith: What's that supposed to mean?
Archmage_Ged: Just what I said.
Sam_Goldsmith: I don't see how you can help when you won't tell me who you are.

This was just too weird.

Sam_Goldsmith: Signing off now.

Archmage_Ged: Wait, don't.

And for some reason, with that, I had the sense that I really was talking to Hayden. I mean, I knew it was impossible, and yet it sounded so much like him, teasing me for a while but quick to get serious, especially if he could tell I was getting annoyed at him. My heart started racing.

Sam_Goldsmith: Are you ready to be straight with me now? Who are you?
Archmage_Ged: I'm Archmage_Ged.

Interesting. He hadn't said he was Hayden.

Sam_Goldsmith: Prove it.

The cursor blinked. The air in the room seemed to grow colder, and the goose bumps rose on my arms again. I looked at the clock on my computer screen. Somehow it was two in the morning. I'd been sitting here for hours and hadn't even realized it. Hell, I was probably hallucinating; I'd barely slept in days, and it didn't look like I'd be making up any ground tonight.

And then, all of a sudden, a song began playing, the music streaming through my computer speakers.

It was that Skylar Grey song I'd never heard before from the playlist. But the playlist had stopped playing hours ago.

The room had been quiet since I paused the game. The song felt almost like an assault on the silence.

Archmage_Ged: See?

Sam_Goldsmith: That doesn't tell me anything. I don't even know that song.

It was some chick I'd never heard before, and I had no idea why Hayden would be listening to her.

Archmage_Ged: That's the whole point. There's a lot you don't know. But I want you to.

Sam_Goldsmith: So tell me!

But the cursor just kept blinking.

Sam_Goldsmith: Are these songs supposed to mean something? Seems pretty obvious to play me some dumb chick music about invisibility when I can't even see you.

Archmage_Ged: Lots of people want to be invisible. Maybe they even think they can pretend to be. But someone always sees.

Now the hairs on my neck were standing up. I must have looked like a plucked chicken. A scared, probably hallucinating chicken. But the thing was, whoever this Archmage_Ged was sounded an awful lot like Hayden. Especially because I had no idea what he was talking about.

Archmage_Ged: You'll figure it out.

As if he'd read my mind.

5

"ONE"

METALLICA

ARCHMAGE_GED HAD ME SO FREAKED OUT that I got almost no sleep the whole weekend, and I was terrified to turn on my computer—I wasn't sure whether I wanted the Gchat window to pop up again. In the light of day it seemed clear to me that there was no way it could have been Hayden. Better to focus on things that were real, like the fact that I had to go to school.

For my first day back I put on my favorite jeans, a zip-up hoodie, and my Metallica T-shirt—one of their songs had come on the playlist as I was getting ready, and it made me think of Hayden. They were one of the bands we fought about; Hayden was strongly in favor of their stance against music piracy, but I wasn't so sure. "What if you spent your whole life working for something and people thought they were entitled to it for free?" he said. He didn't have to add that he thought I'd understand, as someone who didn't have a lot of money, but I knew he was thinking it. He always tried to be sensitive about the fact that his family was loaded and mine wasn't, but sometimes there was no getting around it.

"If I was already a billionaire then maybe it wouldn't be such a big deal," I said. "And it's not like most of the money is going to the artists anyway. It's all about making record companies rich. It costs nothing to distribute music electronically—this stuff should be dirt cheap by now."

As usual, though, I was pretty sure Hayden was right. God, I missed fighting with him.

I walked downstairs to grab some coffee before school. Mom was sitting at the kitchen table in her scrubs, both hands wrapped around an enormous mug of what smelled like tea as I walked down the stairs. Tea meant she'd just gotten home from work and was about to go to bed. It was so weird to be on such different schedules. She gave me an up-and-down look as I headed toward the coffeepot, which she always put on for me and Rachel even though she never had any. She could be pretty cool like that. "Is that what you're wearing?" she asked.

"Something wrong with it?"

She opened her mouth, paused, closed it, opened it again. "No," she said finally. "I'll see you at dinner tonight, and you can tell me all about your first day back, all right? And make sure to be on time—apparently Rachel is bringing a friend home."

"A friend?"

"A gentleman caller," Mom said, with one eyebrow arched.

"This should be good." Rachel had horrible taste in boyfriends, and there had been a lot of them. Most of them never made it past the driveway, though, so she must be really into this one.

"Indeed. Now get to school—you don't want to be late."

That was debatable, but I left just in time to catch the bus, where I sat alone in one of the front seats, listening to my iPod. That was normal—I always sat alone. It wasn't that I wanted to, necessarily, but for some reason it seemed terrifying to just sit down next to a random person. Was I supposed to talk to them? What would I say? As long as I could remember I'd been shy around strangers—not as bad as Hayden, but bad enough. I was fine once I knew someone, but I hadn't really gotten to know anyone except Hayden, at least since I moved to Libertyville. I'd counted myself lucky to have made such a good friend, someone who made me stop feeling so lonely, and for years that was enough. Until it wasn't anymore.

I'd imagined that everything would be different once Hayden and I got to high school. I felt like we'd both made progress in getting over our shyness; now we'd have a chance to expand our insular little world. In high school, I was sure, there would be a bunch of guys more like us—into gaming and music, maybe a little geeky but not total dorks—and they'd be our friends. Maybe there would even be some girls. Girls like Astrid.

And some of that had been true. Libertyville High was huge—it had kids not just from Libertyville itself but from a bunch of neighboring farm towns, and there were tons of kids who neither of us had ever met, some of whom looked like us and ran clubs that included stuff we were into. Gaming, comics, all that. But I'd counted on Hayden being on the same page as me, and as soon as school started, I could tell I'd been wrong. I couldn't get Hayden to come with me to anything, and I was too nervous to go alone.

I figured out pretty quickly why Hayden was so inclined to hide out. Ryan and his friends were in my sister's grade, so they were all juniors by the time we got to school. But Rachel was content to pretend she was an only child, ignoring me when we ran into each other in the halls. Not Ryan. We'd made it through the first few days of school without incident, happy in the knowledge that even though we didn't have any classes together—I was in the Honors track, but Hayden was dyslexic and stuck in all the lower-level classes—we shared a lunch period most days. And on Fridays, we shared it with Ryan and his friends.

"Oh, look, it's Ryan's fatass little brother," we'd heard Trevor say as we sat down with our lunches.

"How are you liking the new school, Gayden?" Jason said, plunking his tray down next to Hayden. That was their second-favorite nickname for him. The first was an oldie-but-goodie, one Ryan had come up with when they were little kids: Hate-him.

"Leave me alone," Hayden said, looking around for Ryan. Sad that he'd thought Ryan might be able to help. He realized his mistake as soon as he saw Ryan standing right behind Jason, laughing. "Not funny, Ryan."

"Oh, I don't know," Ryan said. "It's kind of funny."

"Maybe he's right," Trevor said. "Maybe we need to step up our game." He opened up his little box of chocolate milk and dumped it over Hayden's head. The three of them started laughing.

"That's definitely funny," Ryan said.

I'll never forget the look on Hayden's face as he sat there, milk dripping down onto his favorite T-shirt. Metallica, like the one I wore now. I saw the knowledge wash over him that nothing was going to change, that things would perhaps be even worse than he'd thought. That Ryan wasn't going to help him. And as the sound of people laughing grew louder, once the other kids saw what had happened, I realized he was probably right.

I thought about that moment as I stepped into the cafeteria for the first time since Hayden died. I'd spent most of the morning nodding off in my classes, but there was this kind of protective bubble around me—I could tell none of the teachers wanted to say anything to me because of Hayden. The kids were friendlier, though—people said hi to me in the halls who'd never spoken to me before, and some even complimented my T-shirt. This strange attention from people who used to ignore me was confusing. It was almost as if they were treating me like a celebrity. Best-friend-of-dead-guy = famous. Like it was some kind of accomplishment.

Before, everyone pretty much had left me alone. I didn't fit into any of the groups—I wasn't a grind like the brainiacs in my classes, who looked down on Hayden because they thought he was stupid; I was too uncoordinated for sports but big enough to be hard to knock over; I wasn't artsy or creative or talented at anything; it turned out that the kids in the gaming club were way too dorky, and they weren't into music like Hayden and I were. And the kids who were into the music we liked looked down on anyone who was into gaming. We couldn't win.

Anyone who was anyone at this school fit in somewhere, even if the lines were fluid—jock brainiacs were still cool, the kids who had the best drugs could hang out with anyone, that sort of thing. Parties were fair game for anyone as far as I knew, though Hayden and I hadn't ventured into that scene very much. Until we did, and look where that had gotten us. No, after that day in the cafeteria I'd figured out it was safest to stick with Hayden, and apparently the whole school agreed with me. Some days I wondered whether, if it wasn't for him, I would ever talk to a single person.

Now I was a spectacle. I put in my earbuds so I wouldn't have to hear people talking about me as I walked through the cafeteria with my tray, nodding occasionally to the random people who waved as if they knew me. I headed for the table in the back where I used to sit with Hayden, looking for Astrid as I went. I thought I remembered seeing flashes of her blond hair at lunch before, but it might have just been wishful thinking, because I made it to the table without seeing her. I sat down and forced myself to doctor up a hot dog as best as I could, drowning it in ketchup, mustard, and relish to hide the sight of its unnatural pinkness. Which meant that condiments squirted everywhere as soon as my teeth clamped into the roll. I could feel the bright green relish dribbling down my face and onto the Metallica T-shirt. At least I was alone. One of the perks of having no friends was that no one was there to see you squirt condiments all over yourself.

Except I wasn't really alone. "Do you have any idea what's in those things?" Astrid said, from over my shoulder.

I finished chewing and grabbed a napkin to wipe off the relish. Astrid plunked herself down in the seat across from me. Way to make an impression, Sam, I thought, but what did it matter? She had that hipster boyfriend anyway. "I try not to think about it," I said.

"That's probably for the best. First day back?"

I nodded, wanting to think of something witty to say, but I had nothing. "Do we have the same lunch period?"

"Looks like it, Captain Obvious." She grinned, but I still felt like an idiot. "Want to come sit with my friends?" She pointed at a table a few rows over and back from where I was sitting. There was a group of kids there I'd seen before, part of the artsy crowd. They spent a lot of time in the studio on the upper level and at a coffee shop in South Branch, the next town over, listening to slam poetry or whatever. It wasn't my scene. I wasn't even sure what slam poetry was.

"No, it's okay," I said, trying to dab at the relish without making more of a mess.

"Why not?" she asked, her eyes narrowing.

Could she not see that I'd just made a total mess of myself? I tried to think of something normal to say. "Um, new people, you know. Not sure I'm ready. I mean," I panicked, "not you or anything. I just—" I could tell I wasn't succeeding at trying to sound normal.

"I get it," she said, tugging at a red streak I hadn't remembered being in her hair the other day. I wondered how she knew exactly where it was until I realized it was an extension. How awesome, to be able to change the color of your hair whenever you wanted. She was wearing bright red lipstick to match and it made her eyes look almost unnaturally green. "You should give them a chance sometime, though. They kind of adopted me when I needed some new friends."

She didn't have to add "like you do"—it was implied. I wondered why she'd have needed new friends, but I wasn't sure how to ask. I looked back over at the table and saw Eric sitting there. Great.

"Don't get all judgmental because they're into different stuff than you are. I'll tell you the same thing I told Hayden: I bet you have more in common with some of them than you think."

Instantly I felt a burst of jealousy, which was ridiculous. Like retroactively, as if Hayden had already found better, cooler friends and left me behind.

Except that's not how he'd left me behind. His way was worse.

"How did you know him?" I asked. I guess the easiest way was just to say it.

"Hayden?" She hesitated. "Oh, you know. From around. School, you know."

But Hayden wasn't really around. And I was sure he'd have told me if someone like her was in his classes. Was she even in the same grade as us? For some reason she didn't want to tell me how she knew him, but I had no idea why.

"Come over and sit," she said, still twirling her hair extension. "Maybe you need new friends too." She must have seen the look on my face, though, because she added, "I'm not trying to get you to replace Hayden."

"I know," I said. I didn't want her to think I wasn't interested, but I just couldn't handle meeting a whole bunch of new people. I wasn't feeling ready yet. It was confusing enough just meeting her. "But not today, okay? Some other time?"

"I'll hold you to that," she said, though I wasn't sure she

really meant it until she added, "There's a party Friday night. Give me your phone."

"Anyone ever tell you you're kind of bossy?" I said, but I handed my phone over. Our hands touched as she took it from me, and I could swear I felt a spark. It was probably just static.

She smiled again, and the jewel in her lip ring glittered. "All the time. See you Friday."

I didn't want her to leave, though. "So I watched that movie you told me about? *Donnie Darko*?"

"And? What did you think?" She leaned forward and looked right at me. It seemed like she actually cared what I thought.

Except now I had to say something interesting. I wasn't sure what, but I'd brought it up, so I had to say *something*. Still—time travel, giant rabbits? It was kind of hard to follow. I knew the main character ultimately died, but he wasn't unhappy about it, and I wondered if that's why she'd suggested it. "It was weird. I think I liked it, but I'm not really sure why."

Astrid laughed. She had a great laugh—not some stupid giggle, but a real laugh. I bet Eric could always tell when he was really being funny, and I felt jealous again. "It's a wacky movie. But I figured you like sci-fi stuff, right? And something about the way he accepted what he had to do, it made him seem brave. Like how I thought Hayden was."

Hayden? Brave? "Really?" I asked. I tried not to sound too

skeptical, but I wasn't sure we were talking about the same person. Especially not after what he'd just done.

She shrugged. "That's just how I saw him. He took a lot of crap from people, but he always seemed so, I don't know, stoic about it. I always thought he hadn't let it get him down. Guess I was wrong, though."

The thing was, she wasn't wrong. That had always been my take, too. I just hadn't thought of that as bravery. It just seemed like he'd put up a wall so he wouldn't have to deal with what was happening. And, of course, I hadn't factored in that everyone has a breaking point.

"Did you buy that figurine?" Astrid asked. All these questions she was asking—I'd never had someone take such an interest in my life before. Certainly not a girl.

"Yes." I was tempted to tell her about the other night, but I didn't want her to think I was crazy. Not when it seemed like we were on the verge of actually being friends. "It was a good idea. Thanks."

"No problem," she said. "Glad to help out."

I wondered again how she understood things so well, what she'd been through that made her seem to automatically get it. Or was that just her? I desperately wanted to know more. And though there was something that felt kind of disloyal in thinking so much about another person after I'd just lost my best friend, I had to think Hayden would have approved. He'd liked her too, after all. Though I wasn't sure how much. Why hadn't he introduced us?

The bell rang, signaling the start of fifth period. Astrid looked at the disgusting remains of my hot dog, post–condiment explosion. "I'm sorry I kept you from eating your lunch. And it looks so . . . appetizing." Was I crazy, or did she seem not that sorry?

I picked up a damp, cold french fry and made a spectacle of chomping on it, glad to have the distraction. "What a waste of a delicious meal," I said, then decided to be bold. Maybe it was the sleep deprivation finally getting to me, but the words came out of my mouth before I could overthink it. "Someday I'll introduce you to the best french fries in Libertyville." My face felt hot and I prayed I wouldn't start sweating.

"You're sure I haven't met them yet? I consider myself something of a french fry expert."

"Positive," I said.

"Someday, then," she said with a wink, and then she walked away.

6

"PUMPED UP KICKS"

FOSTER THE PEOPLE

USUALLY FIFTH PERIOD WAS MY English class, but I'd gotten a note in homeroom saying I needed to go meet with the school guidance counselor. I'd met Mr. Beaumont at some meetings the school made us have when we were freshmen, to get us thinking about what kinds of electives we'd want to take. I remembered him being a little guy, a lot shorter than me, dressed more casually than the other administrators, in jeans and a sweater. I figured he was trying to make students think he was cool, though it seemed like maybe he was trying too hard.

He was expecting me; the door was open when I got to his office and he was standing near it, hand outstretched. "Hi, Sam," he said, and waited for me to shake. Weird to have a school official shaking hands, but whatever, so I did it. "Nice to see you again. Have a seat."

His office didn't look like any office at school I'd ever

seen. There was a desk, but it was pushed over into the corner, and in the middle of the room were two big chairs that actually looked pretty comfortable, with a small coffee table between them, and a candy dish filled with M&M's. I'd only eaten that one french fry and catastrophic bite of hot dog, so I was starving.

Mr. Beaumont must have seen me notice them. He sat down in one of the chairs and said, "Take as many as you want. Need some water?"

I sat in the chair across from him, stuffed a handful of M&M's in my mouth, and shook my head. This had the added benefit of saving me from having to say anything right away, since I didn't really see the point of me being here.

"I wanted to reach out to you, see how you're doing," he said. "You know, we're all devastated by what happened, as I'm sure you are. It might make you feel better to talk about it."

Not a chance. "I don't see how," I said.

"I'm sure it must seem that way right now. But can we just try? Maybe it'll help, maybe it won't, but either way, we'll know."

I shrugged. Obviously he wasn't going to let me out of here until I said something.

"I understand you two were very close," Mr. Beaumont said.

"That's one way of putting it," I said.

"What's another way?"

I shrugged. How was I supposed to describe my relationship with Hayden? He was my best friend. My only friend. And I'd thought it might be time for that to change, and he hadn't, and now he was gone. I wasn't about to sit here for however long he made me stay and get into that.

"Can you describe your friendship to me at all?" he asked gently.

What did he expect me to say? That we were both socially awkward misfits? That we'd saved each other from loneliness for a really long time, and now that was over? "We were friends. What else am I supposed to say?" My knee was bouncing up and down, almost as if I had no control over it. I really didn't want to be here.

"Was he your only friend?"

Now my knee was even more out of control. I willed it to stop shaking before Mr. Beaumont noticed. "I guess."

"And you were his? Only friend?" His voice was getting quieter and quieter, as if he knew the questions would be hard to hear, no matter at what volume. But despite him trying to soften me up, I could feel myself getting angry, blood heating up my face. He must have seen it, too, because he didn't wait for me to say anything. "Look, I know it's going to be hard to talk about Hayden. I'll give you some things to read for later on, when you feel like it." He gave me a manila envelope. I didn't bother opening it, just stuck it in my backpack.

"I understand you're probably sad and confused, and probably angry, too. I want you to know it's okay to feel anything you're feeling right now."

Great, now I had permission. I was about to say something snarky, but that was still an invitation to talk, and I didn't want to talk. Not to Mr. Beaumont, not to anyone.

Mr. Beaumont must have been some kind of mind reader, though. "I see that you're not eager to talk to me about this, and that's fine. I want to be a resource for you, but only if you want me to be. I do think it would help you to talk to someone, though, so maybe we could talk about who that might be?"

He knew how to find the soft spots. I couldn't really talk to Mom; she was so busy at work with all those extra shifts, and no matter what I said she'd worry, and she was worried enough already. Rachel wouldn't be any help, and though Astrid had the potential to be a new friend, I didn't want to think about her as a confidante, not like this. There wasn't really anyone else. I looked down at the floor. Mr. Beaumont had put a big Persian rug over the gray industrial carpeting. He was trying pretty hard. "There's no one else," I said finally.

"Well, if that's the case, I hope you'll at least consider me as an option," he said. "Maybe we can talk a little less about Hayden and a little bit more about you, for now? I can stop trying to guess how you're feeling if you just tell me."

"I'll try," I said. But it was hard to narrow it down. There was the anger/guilt/missing cycle, with a whole bunch of other emotions thrown in there, which was kind of hard to describe. "It's a big jumble, I guess. It doesn't seem real. I keep thinking he'll be here soon, and he won't." My knee was starting to bounce again, so I hooked my foot around the leg of the chair to make it stop.

Mr. Beaumont nodded. "I lost a friend when I was very young. And I remember thinking the same thing—I kept waiting for him in places I expected him to be, or getting extra cookies at lunch because I'd always pick some up for him. But it does get easier, with time."

If he was just going to trot out the clichés, talking to him would be useless. "Yeah, I've heard people say that."

He leaned forward and I could feel him looking at me, though I focused my eyes on the prints he'd hung up on the wall. All abstract stuff, but in soothing colors. The whole office was kind of cheesy. "People are going to say a lot of things. And some of it will be helpful, and some of it will be annoying, and lots of it will get on your nerves. But they're saying it because people said those things to them, or because they found it helpful when they lost someone. They mean well."

Sure they did. "Is that supposed to make it better?" I looked him right in the eyes then and hoped he couldn't see what I was thinking.

He met my gaze and somehow I felt like he knew, and that it didn't bother him. "Not yet," he said. "Someday."

I knew he was trying to help, but he was dead-on about the whole getting-on-my-nerves thing. "Is that all?" I started to stand up.

He held up a hand. "Can I have just a couple of minutes more? I was hoping maybe you could tell me whether Hayden confided in you about how he was feeling. Did you have a sense that he was thinking about doing this?"

Way to jump right into it. I sat back down. What was I supposed to say? We talked about it all the time, but I never thought he was serious. I never was. "Any kid who's been picked on as much as Hayden has thought about it," I said.

"So he did talk to you?"

Talked about it? It was a running joke with us. We'd spent hours playing with Hayden's iPhone, trying to get Siri, the virtual personal assistant, to recommend a suicide hotline. "I'm depressed, Siri," Hayden would say.

I don't understand, Hayden.

"I need help, Siri."

I don't understand, Hayden.

"I'm lonely. I don't have any friends."

I'm really tired of these arbitrary categories, Hayden.

"Siri, are you mad at me?"

No comment, Hayden.

We'd kept asking questions until we couldn't talk because

we were laughing so hard. Eventually we figured out we just needed to be more direct. "Siri, I want to jump off a bridge . . . which one is the tallest?"

But not for a second did I think he meant it. *I* never had. I knew things were bad—I couldn't put that party out of my mind, no matter how hard I tried—but I had no idea he'd take it to this extreme. I figured he'd lock himself in his room for the weekend and ignore me, like he did sometimes when he was upset, or when I'd been a jerk, or both. I'd text him jokes and invite him to Gchat, but I wouldn't hear from him until later in the week, maybe, and then only in Mage Warfare. He'd use his archmage powers to take down some really big creatures and I'd know that he'd gotten his revenge.

Only on some level I must have known that this time was different. After all, I'd gone to his house the next morning instead of following our normal routine.

"Sam?"

"Sorry," I said, shaking my head. "I spaced out for a second. I haven't been sleeping much."

"Understandable. So you were saying that Hayden had mentioned suicide in the past?"

"Not in like a serious way. I didn't see this coming at all." Which was true, mostly.

"Not at all? So there was nothing that might be a triggering event, of sorts?" He was leaning forward again, hands on his thighs, anxious to hear what I had to say.

But there was no way I was going to talk about the party, or anything that had happened since. Hayden had been through enough, and so had I. And I was starting to get angry again. "Look, Hayden was pretty miserable. His brother and his friends treated him like shit, he was bombing all his classes, and I don't know if you've had the pleasure of meeting his parents, but they were awful too. And no one here did anything to make it better. There was a time when maybe someone could have helped him, but it's too late now, so why are you talking to me about it? Why don't you talk to all of them?" My face was burning now, and I realized I was yelling.

"I'm sorry we didn't see what was happening, Sam, and certainly I'll be talking to some of the people you've mentioned. But it's you and me talking now, and I want you to know that I'm here whenever you need me. I know you're angry, and I want to help you channel that anger into something productive, rather than something harmful." He looked like he was going to reach over and touch my arm or something like that, but he must have figured out that I was itching to hit something.

"What do you want me to do? Take art classes and draw pictures using black crayons? Write short stories about an alternative universe where my best friend didn't kill himself? What do you want?" I had to calm down. I tried focusing on my breathing. In, out. In, out. Slower each time.

"I just want you to remember that you have options. Sometimes when people are angry they lash out at other people, and there's enough violence around here as it is." His brows were furrowed, and his voice had gotten quiet again, despite my yelling.

It took me a minute to figure out what he was so worried about. And then I got it. He thought I was going to shoot up the school or something. Hayden had put a song about it on the playlist; I wondered if that meant he'd thought about it himself. I forced myself to stop yelling, to speak almost as quietly as he had. "Look, it's true that I think there are a lot of people to blame for all of this, but I'm one of them." For a second, my mind flashed back to the party, to the last words I'd ever said to him. *Fuck you, Hayden.* Some kind of best friend I was. "And it's not my job to decide who should pay."

Mr. Beaumont exhaled; I hadn't realized he'd been holding his breath. "I'm glad to hear you feel that way, though I'm sorry you feel responsible. Maybe that's something we could talk about next time."

I figured that meant there had to be a next time, so I nodded and took another handful of M&M's before I left.

"In the meantime, get some rest," Mr. Beaumont said. "You look exhausted."

No kidding.

7

"I DON'T WANT TO GROW UP"

THE RAMONES

I WAITED UNTIL I GOT HOME to look at the envelope Mr. Beaumont had given me, once I'd shut myself up in my room. It was full of pamphlets—on suicide, grieving, depression, anger management. The suicide one was loaded with statistics. Someone died by suicide every fourteen minutes or so, which seemed crazy high to me, and a million people a year attempted it. It was the third leading cause of death for teenagers, and boys did it more often than girls. Girls tended to use it as what the pamphlet called a "cry for help," though it sounded more like an attention grab to me. They would slit their wrists but cut the wrong way, or take a bunch of pills when they knew someone was likely to find them. Boys were more definitive. Hanging, shooting, jumping off tall things.

I could just imagine Mr. Beaumont giving a pamphlet like this to Ryan. He'd probably jump all over the fact that Hayden had used a girl's strategy. Leave it to the bully trifecta to come up with reasons to mock him even after he was gone.

The lack of sleep was starting to make me dizzy so I lay down on my bed for a while and tried to take a nap. But my head was still spinning from all the different things going on—Hayden being gone, of course, but also Astrid, and the Archmage. Except I was pretty sure I must have dreamed the Archmage. I wasn't in the habit of falling asleep in my desk chair, but there was a first time for everything. I tried to put it out of my head but just when I thought I was about to drift off there was a knock at the door.

"Mom, I'm trying to sleep in here."

"It's not Mom." I opened my eyes. The door opened and Rachel came in my room wearing her usual outfit: a very tiny skirt and so much makeup it looked like she'd spray-painted it on. Funny, when she didn't have on a fake face she and Mom looked a lot alike—both were tall, with long brown curly hair and big brown eyes. But while Mom looked tired all the time from working, Rachel looked like she worked at one of the makeup counters at the mall. Which was actually her dream job. All that makeup made her look old, though, almost as old as Mom. If she just took off half of the makeup and gave it to Mom, they'd both look great.

Not that I'd ever say that to either one of them. I wasn't a complete idiot.

"You haven't stepped one foot in my room in at least a year," I pointed out. "What are you doing here?"

She looked around at the band posters that covered every inch of the walls not already taken over by my bookshelves. "It hasn't improved much. Listen, Jimmy's coming over for dinner and I need you to get your ass downstairs ASAP and make this as painless as possible."

"I totally forgot," I said, and closed my eyes again. "Mom said something this morning. I think I'll just stay up here."

I felt the weight of Rachel sitting down on the edge of my bed, which was weird enough that I opened my eyes again.

"She probably didn't tell you she's decided to cook," Rachel said, wrinkling her nose. "There are so many ways this could turn into a complete disaster that counting them is making my head explode. I need you to get my back on this one, little brother." She looked at me with what I could only assume she intended as puppy-dog eyes. All I could see were cracks in the makeup as she widened her eyes as far as they could go.

Still, Rachel almost never let herself get into a situation where she owed me a favor. This could be fun. I stood up slowly, feeling pretty dizzy. "You owe me big," I said. "But I must have misunderstood you. You said Mom's cooking? Does she want you guys to break up?"

"That might be the strategy. Cover for me for a bit, okay?"

She disappeared down the hall, and I was left to face the prospect of Mom in the kitchen all by myself. Jimmy was already sitting at the kitchen table by the time I got downstairs. I'd never met him—Rachel had never invited any of her boyfriends to anything involving the family, and this one didn't go to Libertyville High. As soon as I saw him, I understood why she'd never brought him around: he looked like any parent's worst nightmare. Tattoos, stretched earlobes, studded leather jacket, the whole thing. I'd have expected someone who looked like him to be lounging, cigarette dangling from the corner of his mouth even if he was smart enough not to smoke inside. But Jimmy was sitting straight up in his chair, hands folded in front of him like he was at a business meeting. Mom was at the stove, stirring something in a pot billowing with smoke, which was already making me nervous.

Jimmy stood up and held out his hand. "How you doing, man?"

"Not too bad." I shook his hand. His grip was firm, but he didn't do that thing guys do sometimes where they almost crush you so you know how manly they are. "So you're here for dinner, huh?"

Jimmy nodded and tried not to look worried.

"I hope Rachel warned you to eat first," I said.

"Not nice," Mom called out.

"Need some help over there?" I asked.

She turned around and I could see beads of sweat on her forehead. "I might just take you up on that, Sammy."

I hated it when she called me that, especially in front of

Jimmy. It almost made me wish I hadn't offered. But I didn't want her to burn the house down; we'd avoided fires in the past, but narrowly. There was a macaroni-and-cheese incident that I was still trying to forget, and some stains in the ceiling brought back memories of exploding eggs every time I looked up.

I walked over to the stove and looked into the pot, waving away the smoke to see a sludge of white and brown and black, though I couldn't identify anything that actually looked like food. "What is that?" I asked, wrinkling my nose.

"It was supposed to be risotto," Mom said. "With mushrooms and—"

She was interrupted by the smoke alarm. I reached over and shut off the burner, then took the pot and put it in the sink while Mom disabled the alarm. I hoped Jimmy wouldn't notice that we had a system. "What do you like on your pizza, Jimmy?" I asked.

Rachel laughed behind me. I turned and saw she'd changed into a slightly longer skirt, taken off a little bit of the makeup. She looked just respectable enough to make Mom happy. She must really like this guy. "Nice outfit," I said.

"Jerk." She pinched my arm, hard, reactivating the soreness from the bruising, but it made me kind of happy—she used to do that when we were younger, when I'd follow her around just to get her to pay attention to me. Negative attention from her was just as good as positive, when I was little.

"I can eat anything," Jimmy said.

Mom sighed and went to get her wallet.

"Sausage and peppers it is," I said, and went to call it in. We weren't exactly kosher. Sausage and peppers was my favorite; Rachel usually lobbied for Hawaiian, but I figured she wasn't about to fight with me in front of her new boyfriend.

After I hung up I sat at the kitchen table with Jimmy while Rachel helped Mom scrape the burned risotto off the bottom of the pot. We sat and stared at each other for a while. It felt like he was waiting for me to say something, but Rachel must have warned him that I'm not exactly the world's best conversationalist. "Rachel says you're into music," he said finally.

I nodded, though I was surprised she'd told him something so positive, at least compared to what I would have imagined she'd say.

"What are you listening to these days?" he asked. I'd changed from my relish-crusted Metallica shirt into a vintage Coca-Cola T-shirt I'd found at a thrift store. "Mostly alternative stuff, am I right?"

I leaned back in my chair and crossed my arms. Yeah, he was right, but who was he to judge me just on my clothes? Had he looked in the mirror lately? "The Ramones, right now." It was sort of true; it was what had been on the playlist when I'd listened to it on my way home from school.

"Good stuff. I've been digging the Clash lately, myself. I'll burn *London Calling* for you if you don't have it already. You'll like it."

That was actually pretty cool of him. Maybe he wasn't as bad as I thought.

Mom and Rachel came back in and started setting the table with paper plates and plastic silverware. As if we were really going to cut up our pizza. "So how'd you get into the Ramones?" Jimmy asked.

Rachel snorted. "Since when do you listen to the classic stuff?" She turned to Jimmy. "I made him listen to every album I ever bought and the only stuff of mine he ever liked was indie."

To his credit, Jimmy didn't change his facial expression at all. "It's all about variety, man," he said, and held out his fist.

What the hell. I bumped fists with Jimmy and said exactly what I was thinking. "I started listening to the Ramones because Hayden put them on his suicide-note playlist."

The kitchen got really quiet, and I knew right away I'd gone too far.

"Sammy, now might not be the time," Mom said finally.

"No, it's cool, Mrs. Goldsmith," Jimmy said. "I kinda went through something similar myself."

"You did?" I asked, before I could help myself. I wondered if Rachel had known. Mom and I both looked over at her. Mom's mouth was hanging open.

Rachel shrugged, but she didn't look that surprised.

"I moved here from Chicago last summer," Jimmy said. "I had this friend who was going through some stuff, and he offed himself. In my house, with my dad's gun. I'm the one who found him."

For a second I found myself thankful that Hayden had chosen the method he did. I couldn't imagine my last memory of him involving blood. It made me nauseous just thinking about it. I looked over at Rachel again; now she looked a little shocked. I figured she'd known the basics but not the details.

"It's why we left," he continued. "None of us could stand to be in that house, and my mom kept saying how terrible it was to live in cities, all the awful things that happened there."

"Kind of ironic, that you'd move here, and then . . ." My voice trailed off. I wasn't quite ready to say it out loud.

"Yeah, that's one word for it. It would have been a lot harder if I hadn't already met your sister." He smiled at Rachel, and she smiled back. I could see how into him she really was. Even Mom was starting to warm to him. "I loved Chicago—I just wanted to leave the house, not the city. It was my dad's idea to take off for cow country."

"Corn, not cows," Rachel said, and squeezed his hand. I'd been tempted to say the same thing, but let's face it, there were some cows.

"Anyway, I couldn't talk to anyone about it back home, and I didn't really want to talk about it here, but now that it's been a little while I can think about it more clearly. So if you ever need to talk, you can talk to me. Maybe not now, but someday." I wondered if my sister had put him up to it, but that would be so not like her. And he looked like he really meant it.

"That's a very nice offer, Jimmy," Mom said.

I could see Rachel trying not to smirk. This couldn't have gone better if she'd scripted it herself. She looked over at me, willing me to say something.

"Okay, thanks," I said. I was starting to like him, despite myself. Too bad he hadn't showed up before Mr. Beaumont. Then I could have at least said I had someone else to talk to.

The doorbell rang before we could say anything else. Finally, food. It seemed like everyone was grateful to have the pizza to focus on for a while.

"Tell me about your first day back," Mom asked, after we'd all started eating.

"No big deal," I said. I really did not want to talk about Mr. Beaumont.

"You missed last week when everyone was talking about Hayden," Rachel said. "Now they're all talking about what happened to Jason Yoder."

I turned to her so fast I almost hurt my neck. "What happened to Jason?"

"You didn't hear? This rumor started going around that he's gay, I guess. And then, no one knows exactly what happened, but the police found him tied to a telephone pole outside the Blue Star bar. Buck naked. He didn't press charges or anything—I guess he hoped no one would find out. But people always do. Everyone's talking about it."

Libertyville was a pretty conservative town. Even though Iowa was progressive in being one of the first states to legalize gay marriage, it hadn't trickled down to us quite yet. I hadn't heard the rumor about Jason, but that wasn't surprising—I wasn't exactly clued in enough to be part of the rumor mill. But I'd heard about the Blue Star bar. It wasn't officially a gay bar, but in the scheme of our small town, it basically was.

The idea of Jason Yoder—one macho third of the bully trifecta—being tied naked to a telephone pole was a weird image. It was probably his worst nightmare.

"Rachel, there's no need for that kind of gossip," Mom said. "That poor boy."

"Poor boy?" I said, feeling myself getting angry yet again. "He was a total bully who treated Hayden like crap. I'm not sorry."

"Sam!" Mom snapped. "You don't have to like him, but you shouldn't say something like that."

"What's to be sorry about, anyway?" Rachel said. "You didn't do it."

"Of course not. I just meant I'm not sorry it happened to him. That guy was an asshole."

"Language, Sam!" Mom said. "And besides, we're not the kind of family who wishes bad things on other people."

Maybe *you're* not, I wanted to say, and I could see Rachel was thinking the same thing.

8

"DIANE YOUNG"

VAMPIRE WEEKEND

AFTER DINNER I WENT BACK UP to my room. I knew I wouldn't be able to sleep right away, so I decided to play Mage Warfare, Archmage or no Archmage. I remembered when Hayden and I had first started playing. We'd talked a lot about the kinds of characters we wanted to create. I'd just read this crazy book about a video game that was supposed to be like reality, where the author had all these theories about why people created characters and acted the way they did in the game world. In the book some of them replicated their lives online—they had the same jobs, drove the same cars, hung out with the same kinds of people. It was like they were living their lives twice. And then there were the others, who went as far in the opposite direction as they could: accountants became movie stars, schoolteachers became rapists, that sort of thing. It was fascinating to me.

Hayden found it disturbing, though. "Both of those

options seem off," he'd said. "It's hard to imagine that people who were so content with their lives would want to be the same way online—they could just be happy in the real world and not bother with the game at all. And does it really make sense that people's fantasies would have no resemblance to their real lives? I mean, if the schoolteachers were killing bratty kids that would be one thing, right?" He thought it made more sense if people were who they were but better. People who had boring jobs but loved karaoke would be the rock stars; beat cops would save the world. He would be tall and handsome and magical, and he'd fight for good. Like the Archmage.

I was more intrigued by the darker aspects of gaming. I kind of liked being a bad guy in a world where no one knew who I was and where there were no consequences. And the whole idea of good and evil—there were so many people everyone thought were good who were clearly awful, so why was it a given that being on the good side was any better than being on the bad one?

"If everyone thought like you did, there would be anarchy," Hayden said.

"I'm not sure that would be the worst thing in the world," I said. "How can you say you believe in good and evil as absolutes and then look at politics? Both sides think they're the good guys, and both seem like idiots to me. And they're totally inconsistent—one side says government is bad but wants to control everything you do, and the other says government is good and then can't get anything done, which makes government look bad. If there were anarchy, people would have to find ways to work together to make anything happen."

"It's crazy to think people would manage without anyone in charge," he said. "Look how desperate most people are for someone to tell them what to do."

"Some people," I said. "But look at us—we both learn way more on our own than we do at school, and we're more interested in things we find for ourselves."

"That's what makes us weird," he said, but he laughed as he said it.

I thought about that conversation a lot, after he was gone. We hadn't talked about the fact that we had different goals in learning on our own: I did it because I could, because I wanted to learn different things than the school wanted to teach me, because I looked forward to the day I could leave Libertyville behind and start over. Mom always reminded me that the best years of my life were ahead of me, that for the jerks in high school this was as good as it got, whereas someone like me would move on to more exciting things. "You're going to have a beautiful life," she'd say, smoothing my hair with her cool hand, "and high school will be just a distant memory."

But Hayden learned things on his own because he was having trouble learning them any other way. I couldn't imagine how frustrating it must have been to be as smart as he was—brilliant, even—but to have trouble getting his thoughts out of his head. He could communicate with me just fine, but the teachers at school made him nervous, and he stammered and sputtered when they asked him questions. His writing wasn't much better; he was okay when we Gchatted, in part because of autocorrect, but when it came to working through his thoughts on paper, the dyslexia got him every time. I realized we hadn't talked much about his plans for the future; whenever I'd asked, he'd shut me down.

Was it possible that he'd always known it would end this way? What else hadn't he told me?

Then a weird thought occurred to me. There *was* someone I could ask.

The Archmage.

Right. I put the thought out of my head and logged in to Mage Warfare, losing myself in the game for hours. I was on fire—I killed so many people I couldn't keep track of all the angry chat messages I was getting. It was like they gave me fuel; the more these random strangers from all over the world cussed me out, the better I did. It didn't matter if the players were good or evil. If they got in my way, they were screwed. I was so wrapped up in the mayhem I'd created that it took me a while to realize that the pinging of the chat window wasn't coming from inside the game.

Archmage_Ged: How do?

It was happening again. And I was sure I was awake—I'd drunk so much Coke with my pizza I might never sleep again, though admittedly I hadn't even begun to make up for the hours I'd lost. I looked at the clock: 1:43 a.m. Later than I realized. I was going to have to call it soon.

Sam_Goldsmith: Whoever this is, cut it out.
Archmage_Ged: You know who this is. Miss me?
Sam_Goldsmith: Seriously, stop it.

And I meant it. Much as I would have loved to talk to Hayden, I didn't believe it was really him. There was no afterlife where people got to come back as their fantasy selves. It didn't even work in Mage Warfare.

Archmage_Ged: Come on, the fun's only just started!

Fun? My best friend was dead and someone was trying to talk to me about fun? That was just mean.

Sam_Goldsmith: I'm logging out now.

But I waited. Despite myself, I was curious about what was really going on here.

Archmage_Ged: Look, I can help you.

Help me with what? Deal with the fact that my best friend was gone? I wasn't seeing it.

Sam_Goldsmith: There's nothing you can do for me.

Archmage_Ged: You'd be surprised what I can do. Don't you wish there are things you'd done differently? Things you'd change?

Of course there were. But there was no way to go back.

Sam_Goldsmith: Can't change anything. It's too late.

Archmage_Ged: Not for everyone.

Sam_Goldsmith: What do you mean?

The cursor blinked while I waited for him to reply.

Archmage_Ged: One down, two to go.

What was that supposed to mean?

And then I remembered what Rachel had said about Jason Yoder. I imagined he'd been terrified of being outed, and there was no more straightforward way of getting outed than to be tied up naked outside a gay bar.

Maybe it wasn't a coincidence.

Sam_Goldsmith: Are you talking about the bully trifecta?

The cursor just blinked, but like last time, a song from the playlist started coming through my speakers. It was a song I had forwarded through every time it came up; I couldn't bear to remember the last time I'd heard it. I tried to shut off iTunes to make the music stop, but somehow it kept playing. I still didn't want to listen to it.

But apparently now I'd have to.

"I don't understand why all of a sudden you, of all people, want to go to a party," I'd said. We were sitting in Hayden's room, surrounded by wall-to-wall Star Wars paraphernalia. No one would ever think a girl lived there, that's for sure. "You hate parties. You get mad every time I try to make you go to one."

"Which is why you owe me," Hayden said. "If I'm asking, it must be important, right?"

"I guess, but I still don't get it."

"What's to get? You're the one who keeps saying we need to hang out with other people." As usual, I couldn't tell whether he was being sarcastic, and it kind of pissed me off. What was so awful about suggesting that we weren't the only two people at Libertyville High worth interacting with? Not to mention that some of those other people might be girls?

"But for no reason?"

"Who says there isn't a reason?" He gave me a half grin, and I knew he wasn't going to tell me. I'd been bugging him about it all day and gotten nothing. It was really frustrating.

"Look, you don't have to tell me everything, but we're going into enemy territory here. Usually that merits an explanation." The party was at Stephanie Caster's house, and she was part of Ryan's crew. We'd never been to one of those parties before; the few we'd gone to were a little less exclusive.

"Ryan's got an out-of-town game tonight. It should be safe."

"That's not the kind of explanation I was looking for, and you know it," I said, still annoyed.

"Well, sometimes life is unfair."

Stupid cryptic rational Hayden. "You're wearing that?" I asked.

He looked down. "What's wrong with what I'm wearing?"

Nothing, really. Jeans, sneakers, and a Vampire Weekend T-shirt. He actually looked all right—maybe he'd even lost a little weight? Had he been trying and I hadn't noticed? "Didn't know you were into those guys, that's all. Aren't they a little poppy for you?" Hayden usually liked sad, whiny music. Vampire Weekend was my thing.

"Maybe I'm feeling more upbeat today."

"Well, good for you," I said. Sure, now he was feeling

upbeat. I'd been trying to get him to go to parties forever, parties with people that we might actually like. And now, the one time he was willing to leave the house, we were stuck with the Stephanie Caster crowd. I knew I should just be grateful that he was willing to branch out, but for some reason it annoyed me. Why did everything have to be on his terms?

"Why are you being such an asshole?" It wasn't like Hayden to get all confrontational. He must have been really excited about the stupid party to get so irritated with me.

"Didn't mean to pee in your Cheerios. Sorry." I got up from sitting on his bed and sat at the desk, scrolling through iTunes on Hayden's fancy MacBook. "Here, you want upbeat? We'll do upbeat." I clicked on "Diane Young." "In honor of your shirt," I said.

"That's pretty aggressively upbeat," he said.

"Lyrics are still a downer, though. Saying someone's got the luck of a Kennedy is harsh."

"Are we going to sit around talking about lyrics all night? We should probably get out of here."

No. I forced myself to snap out of the daze I'd been in. I wasn't at the party with Hayden; I was home, alone, in my room. And I wasn't ready to think about this yet. I tried rebooting the computer to make the music stop, but nothing happened.

The song kept playing, its rapid-fire drumbeat echoing against the walls.

Creepy. Almost creepier because the song was so happy sounding. Almost like it was mocking me.

My Gchat window pinged.

Archmage_Ged: Come on, you can remember the whole thing.

It wasn't going to happen. Not now. I couldn't handle another night without enough sleep; that had to be why all this was happening. None of it was real.

And yet the song kept playing.

I tried shutting down iTunes again, clicking out of Gchat. Nothing.

It sounded as if the song was getting even louder. Which was impossible.

My heart was pounding and when I looked down I realized my hands were shaking. Finally I slammed my laptop shut. The music ended as abruptly as it had begun; the silence seemed almost loud. Loud enough to keep me awake, but I really had to go to sleep.

Except when I turned around, someone was sitting on my bed.

I opened my mouth to scream but nothing came out. The person on the bed was a man, young but not handsome, with long reddish-brown hair that almost matched his skin.

Archmage_Ged.

Or at least someone who looked almost exactly like the wizard figurine I'd bought. I looked up at my shelf—but the figurine wasn't there.

It made no sense. I felt myself starting to panic. How did he get in my room? There was no way this could really be happening.

"Who are you?" I asked, finally, but he didn't say anything. He just looked at me. Then the air around him seemed to shimmer, and the room got cold, almost like there was a breeze blowing in, though my windows were closed. And yet I was sweating.

I closed my eyes and felt my head pounding, almost like my brain was trying to come out my ears. This was not real. It couldn't be.

I tried to monitor my breathing, to keep from panicking. In. Out. In. Out. Slowly. I had to find a way to be rational. Hayden's vision of Archmage_Ged was, I knew, a kind of dashing magician, a glamorous alternative-universe David Blaine. If he were really Archmage_Ged, wasn't that who I would see? I'd always pictured him as more like Gandalf, a tall old man with long gray hair and flowing robes; if this were all my imagination, the person on the bed would look like him.

I was a little calmer now. I opened my eyes again.

The figurine was there.

But the wizard was gone.

9

"SMELLS LIKE TEEN SPIRIT"

NIRVANA

Remember, the party's tonight. Come early.

All day Friday I stared at Astrid's text. She'd really meant it when she said I should come. It was Friday afternoon, and though I hadn't forgotten about the party, I just wasn't sure it was a good idea to go.

I'd spent the rest of the week completely freaked out about the Archmage situation. What had really happened in my room that night? I'd been so wired that I hadn't slept at all, and I'd been up most nights since trying to figure it out. Now I felt like a zombie. I needed to talk to someone about it, but there was no way I would even consider Astrid, and the only other people I could imagine—Mom, Mr. Beaumont, Jimmy—would all think I was crazy. Which I was starting to think I was. No, I had to put it out of my mind. I knew I should probably just stay in, especially given what happened last time I went to a party, but maybe this was the kind of distraction I needed.

Kind of presumptuous of you to assume I'm going, isn't it?

I read it over before I sent it and realized it sounded rude, so I added a winking smiley face and hoped it was enough.

;-)

Oh, you're going. Trust me, it'll be a good thing.

How could I argue with that? I started getting ready. I brushed my teeth so many times my gums bled, and I accidentally put too much gel in my hair and had to wash it twice to get it out. I spent what felt like an hour staring at a drawer of T-shirts, before deciding on a Raygun shirt that said MAKE AWKWARD SEXUAL ADVANCES NOT WAR. Mom had rolled her eyes when I bought it, but I guess she thought the odds were against me getting to make the advances in the first place. She was probably right; I had a feeling the shirt could do more harm than good. But I liked it.

Hayden's mix wasn't exactly filled with party music, but I was finding it hard to listen to anything else these days. I didn't think I'd ever be able to listen to that Vampire Weekend song again, so I opted instead for a song we'd rocked out to together before. It felt a little bit like an homage.

But it made me even more conflicted about whether I should be going out. I couldn't imagine what Hayden would do in my place, but I'd never have put him in this place. And I wouldn't be in this place at all if he were still here. Bitter, maybe, but true.

The party was on my side of town, which was already a point in its favor. The jock jerks tended to stay on their side, where there was always action because their parents traveled so much. "I'm kind of nervous about this," I admitted to Astrid, when she called to give me the details. "I haven't been to that many parties, and the last one . . ." I couldn't finish the sentence. Not out loud.

"I know," she said. "Why don't I come to your house first and we can walk over together? Then maybe you won't feel weird about going."

"That would be great," I said, exhaling. I'd wanted to ask her if we could meet up first, but I'd been too nervous. So much for awkward sexual advances—I couldn't even make awkward friendly advances. "Eric won't mind?"

"Not at all! He can drive us home."

For a second, I'd hoped she'd say that he wasn't coming, that they'd broken up, but I reminded myself that she was my new friend, not my future girlfriend. Even if that might have been nice. Or amazing.

Now I just had to wait for her to show up. Of all nights for Mom to be working the graveyard shift, this was the worst, because she hadn't left the house yet.

"Look at you," she said, and messed up my hair.

I ducked back. "Cut it out!"

"Don't worry, it still looks . . . I'm not sure what it is you're going for here. It still looks messy. Is that what you want?"

"It's not messy," I said. "It's spiked."

"Sweetie, your hair's a little too long for that. But it looks great. Really."

She totally didn't mean it, but I didn't care.

"Now I have to get parental. Where is this party? Who's going to be there? What time are you coming home?" She said it all rapid fire, like she was joking, but I knew she was serious.

I didn't see that it mattered, given that she'd be gone all night, but whatever. I gave her the details I knew and told her I had no idea who would be there or when I was coming back.

"You're just daring me to give you a curfew, aren't you?"

"Would you really do that?" She never had before. Then again, there hadn't been much of a need.

"Do I have to?" She frowned and put her hands on her hips.

She didn't, really—the town already had a curfew of midnight, so it wasn't like I could stay out any later than that. Which I reminded her.

"I guess that will do," she said. "It's already after eight. You should get going."

"I'm waiting for someone." Crap, I could feel myself blushing.

"You are?" Mom looked excited. "That's great! Who?"

"Um," I said, "just someone."

"A male someone or a female someone?" She looked more intrigued than concerned. It was true that I'd never so much as mentioned a girl to her before; we'd had the talk years ago, the first time I'd asked her a question about babies, but other than that we'd steered clear of conversations about dating other than to make fun of Rachel's choice of suitors.

The doorbell rang before I could answer her question. I ran to answer it but Mom was closer and beat me there. "Hello," she said, "I'm Sam's mom. You can call me Sarah. And you are . . . ?"

"Hi, I'm Astrid. Nice to meet you."

She didn't seem at all annoyed to be meeting my mom, which was nice. And she looked fantastic—her whitish-blond hair was down and glittered with silver, gold, and bronze streaks, and she was wearing a silvery top and shiny gold pants and carrying a bronze backpack.

"Is this a costume party?" Mom asked. "I think Sam might be a little underdressed here."

"Mom!" I yelled, but Astrid just laughed.

"No, it's just a regular party. I felt like getting fancy is all.

This isn't the kind of outfit I can wear to school."

"No, you're right about that," Mom agreed. I listened for her tone but she seemed amused. "Well, you're very sparkly."

"That was the goal," Astrid said, and laughed again. "Sam, we should really get going."

"Okay. See you later, Mom." I prayed she wouldn't do something annoying like try to kiss me before I left.

"Have fun," she said. "And make sure to keep your phone on. You never know when I might need you."

I rolled my eyes as I shut the door behind me.

"Your mom's really sweet," Astrid said.

"She's a total pain," I said, but secretly I agreed with her. "What's in the bag?" I pointed to her bulging bronze backpack.

"That's the beer," she said. "It's BYOB. No keg."

I hadn't even thought of that. "I didn't bring anything," I said apologetically.

"No worries. I brought enough to share. I don't drink much, anyway."

My shoulders sagged; I hadn't realized I'd tensed them. "Neither do I."

"Something else we have in common, then," she said.

Was I crazy, or was she flirting with me?

"I like the T-shirt," she said.

I felt myself blushing again. "Thanks."

"You know, you haven't commented on my outfit yet.

Were you going to let your mom take care of that for you? Or do you not like it?" She almost looked worried. Did she really care what I thought?

"No, I do, I mean, I meant to say—" Get it together, Sam. "You look great. Really. Sparkly, like my mom said."

She smiled then, a wide grin that made the gem in her lip ring sparkle in the dim light. She was so pretty, and I liked that it was an odd prettiness, that it wasn't a given that everyone in the world would be able to see it. It made her special. To me, anyway.

The streets were quiet and dark; this part of town didn't have that many streetlights. The party wasn't that far away, so we didn't have to talk much, which was nice; I was too busy trying to figure out how to talk to Astrid. We walked for a few blocks, past the apartment building they'd been trying unsuccessfully to convert to condos for as long as I could remember, past the all-night 7-Eleven where some Mexican dudes in a cart outside sold some of the best tamales I'd ever had, not that I was any kind of expert on authentic Mexican food. The party was in a neighborhood filled with houses just like ours, little run-down one- and two-family setups with too many people crammed into too-small spaces.

"We're almost there," Astrid said, and pointed to a house a block away. I heard the faint strains of music I actually liked blaring from the speakers and I could tell already that it would be a better party than any of the other ones I'd been to, where they played crappy radio dance pop.

When we got to the door, though, I hesitated. I remembered the other night, Vampire Weekend playing in my head, along with the sound of Hayden laughing. Was I really ready for this?

"Come on," Astrid said, and grabbed my hand.

The door opened into the living room; the house was laid out just like mine. It was a nice change from those other parties, where everything felt unfamiliar. Here I could almost feel at home. The room was full of the indie kids Astrid sat with at lunch—a few locals from my side of town, and the artsy kids from South Branch. Emo kids with dyed hair and piercings; skinny hipsters like Eric. I almost looked like I fit in. I almost felt it, too. It was a strange feeling, one I wasn't used to.

We walked through the living room to the kitchen, where Astrid took the beer out of her backpack, pulled out two for us, then stashed the rest in the fridge. We found a bottle opener and pulled off the caps, then clinked our bottles.

"Cheers," I said.

"To a good night," she said.

I took a long sip of beer, almost spitting it out as soon as I remembered how gross it tasted. Maybe someday I'd get used to it, but I didn't see it happening anytime soon.

"Let's meet some people," she said, and steered me through the crowd. "Here's someone I think you'll like. Sam, meet Damian. Damian, Sam. You two get to know each other. I'll be back." She wandered off, greeting people as she went.

Sure, not awkward at all. Especially for the guy who couldn't even talk to people on the bus. I stared at Damian for a minute. "Dig the facial hair," I said. Damian was the first high school student I'd ever seen who'd successfully managed to grow a full beard.

"Thanks, man." He smiled and tugged at the end of it. "Most of it's going to go in Movember."

"Movember?"

"National mustache month. I'm thinking about a Van Buren."

"Van Buren?" Was I only going to be able to manage stupid questions?

"After the president. He had some crazy facial hair going. Big mustache, big puffy sideburns, no beard. Sure to be a hit with the ladies." He pulled out the sides of his beard to show where the sideburns would pouf out.

I liked him immediately. It turned out he was taking extra writing and art classes so he could work on a graphic novel, so we immediately started debating the merits of the *Walking Dead* TV show versus the comic. It was the kind of conversation I used to have with Hayden, and it made me feel happy and lonely at the same time. I wasn't replacing him, was I? We talked long enough for me to force down another couple of beers, which tasted less bitter now.

I felt a poke on my left shoulder and turned toward it, only to find no one there. I heard Astrid laugh from my right side. "That still works on you, huh? Glad to see you two hitting it off."

"It was nice to meet you, Sam," Damian said. "Maybe I'll see you around school?"

"Sure thing," I said, and turned to Astrid. "You're right on both counts. He seems really cool, and I'm very gullible. And possibly a little buzzed." It was true; I was feeling looser, more relaxed. This must have been what people were going for. I could almost understand why people went to parties. Or at least why they tolerated beer.

"From one beer? You really weren't lying about not drinking much. Here, have another one." She handed me a bottle.

"Three, actually. And I don't lie." Which was mostly true.

We walked over to the couch, which was mercifully unoccupied, and sat down. It had seen better days, and the cushions sagged so much I had to restrain myself from sliding into Astrid's lap.

"You don't lie at all, huh?" she said. "So you'll answer any question I ask, truthfully?" Her couch cushion must have been sagging too, because she kept moving closer and closer to me.

"I didn't say that. What about you? Are you a liar?" I meant it to sound flirty, but it came out kind of harsh.

I thought maybe she'd be offended, but instead she

lowered her eyelids. I could see that her eye shadow matched her outfit, all streaks of silver and gold. Even her eyelashes seemed to have gold mascara on them. "I've told some white lies. I try to avoid the whoppers, but sometimes it's just a matter of evasion. How about you test me? Ask me a question."

Well, she was giving me an opening. We were sitting so close now our legs were pressed against each other. "Tell me how you knew Hayden."

She sat straight up and moved fully back onto her own cushion. It was like an invisible curtain had dropped between us. Her hand moved to her head and she started pulling at one of her shiny hair extensions, and I realized she did that when she was nervous.

"After all that, you're not going to tell me?" I asked. "So much for not lying."

"It's not that," she said. "I just want you to have fun at this party, to get your mind off sad things. To not have to think so much about Hayden."

"I don't really think about anything else these days," I said, and that was only a little bit of a lie. Because I'd been thinking about her. A lot. "But if you don't want to tell me, that's fine."

"No, I will." She sighed, and I could tell she was thinking about the day she'd have to do it. I could see the image of bold, confident Astrid slip a little, revealing someone more anxious and nervous underneath. Someone more like me, maybe. "Someday, I promise. Let's just enjoy the party for tonight, though, okay?" She leaned in closer to me, and the room got quiet, almost as if the party itself knew something important was about to happen.

And unfortunately, it did.

"What's up, loser?"

Trevor.

10

"ONE STEP CLOSER"

LINKIN PARK

HE LOOMED OVER THE COUCH, enormous and menacing. I pulled farther away from Astrid, who I could see was getting angry, and stood up. Of course he'd come now, just before it seemed like something was going to happen, even if I didn't know what.

"What are you doing here?" Astrid asked, her eyes narrowed.

"Stay out of it, Alison," he said.

Alison?

"Don't call me that," she said.

What was he talking about? And what was he doing here? This wasn't his kind of party.

"You were out of line at the funeral, you little asshole," he said, and pushed me back down on the couch.

I tried not to flail in the cushions before getting up again, but there was no way to be graceful about it. "So you crashed a party to pick a fight with me? That's your solution?" I could feel the fury growing in me. He was the one who made Hayden's life miserable, and now he was mad at how I'd behaved at the funeral? Seriously? "Look at you—you're a giant. You wouldn't even feel it if I hit you. It's so important to you, to preserve the sanctity of Hayden's funeral, the kid whose life you helped to make a living hell? There wouldn't have even been a funeral if it wasn't for you." Yelling at him was actually making me feel better. I barely noticed that there was a circle of people around us, watching. I wondered what they would do if Trevor really did decide to go after me.

"You're one to talk," he said. "What makes you think you can put it all on me? I saw you at that party, just standing there, watching it all go down. Like you had his back? What makes you such a hero? At least I'm here because I'm looking out for my friend."

"Well, your friend can do just fine on his own. Now he doesn't have an annoying little brother to make him look bad at school. He must be so happy."

Was I trying to make Trevor hit me? I didn't have time to think about it before his fist connected with my cheek; it felt like my face had been turned into a baseball and someone had just hit a home run. It probably only took a second before I was back on the couch again, but it felt like it took ages to land.

"Made your point, Trevor?" I heard Astrid say. "Now get

the fuck out of here." I felt the cushions sag as she sat down next to me. "You okay, Sam?"

I nodded, but I might have been lying. I couldn't tell if I was dizzy from Trevor's knockout punch, or the beers, or the insomnia, but standing up didn't seem like much of an option yet.

"We're not done," Trevor said.

"You really want to threaten me in front of everyone?" I said, but he was already walking away.

I tried to get up and go after him but Astrid put her hand on my leg to stop me, and I was grateful—I still wasn't sure if I could stand up without immediately falling back down. "Let him go," she said. "He'll get his someday. It doesn't have to be now."

"I would have loved to get just one punch in, though. Even if it didn't do any good."

"No need to behave like some dumb guy," she said. She was starting to look pissed off. "I thought you were better than that."

I'd always thought I was, too. But now I was starting to wonder. "I'm not usually like that, I swear," I said. "Look, remember how I said I'd tell you the truth?"

She nodded.

"Let me try it out." I'd never said it out loud before, but now seemed like the right time. "Those guys were at the party, the night Hayden—you know. They were awful to him, like they always were. Worse. And I just stood there, like Trevor said. I didn't do a goddamn thing. I never have. Which means this is all my fault. The only thing that makes me feel better is blaming them. I know it's super hypocritical to have wanted to stand up for myself now, when I never stood up for him, but better late than never, I guess."

Her eyes softened a little. "You know it's not your fault, Sam, right?"

"How can you say that?"

"Tell me what happened," she said.

Stephanie Caster lived just a few blocks away from Hayden, in a house that looked like it came out of a movie. Half the walls were made out of glass; everything else was black, white, or metallic. Angular. Which was ironic, because I'd bet that Stephanie was the least angular girl at Libertyville High. She was a basketball cheerleader with a ridiculous body—curvy everywhere you'd want it to be—who'd been a killer gymnast until the ridiculous body showed up. She was the bendiest person I'd ever seen. And yet she lived in a house where every single thing was square. Or rectangular. Whatever.

"This place is bizarre," I muttered to Hayden, but he wasn't listening. The living room was packed full of people, and he was scanning the crowd. Who was he looking for? His brother and his friends weren't going to be there; it was the only reason I'd agreed to come. I tried not to be annoyed at him for ignoring me; after all, I was the one who'd been pushing him to go out more, so I should have been happy that he was finally willing, right? I'd been getting more and more frustrated with how insular we were, and though we weren't growing apart exactly, Hayden was spending more and more time on the computer, and I wanted to get out and join the world. For the last few weeks he'd wanted to stay in and play Mage Warfare all the time, and I realized that without him I had nothing. No one else to call, no interests that we didn't share. The fact was, I was lonely.

Well, now I was at a party, and Hayden had wandered off to do whatever it was he'd planned to do, and I really was alone, even in a room full of people. This wasn't what I had wanted, not at all.

The keg was in the back of the living room, so I filled a red plastic cup with what seemed like mostly foam and looked around to see if there was anyone I could talk to. But it was mostly basketball and track jocks; the football guys and their friends weren't there, but neither were the more artsy kids that sometimes came to the few parties I'd considered attending. There were some girls from my classes, but the cute ones were there with their boyfriends. Coming here was a mistake. At least I'd learned that going to parties wasn't the answer. I just wanted to go home. I slurped up some foam and looked for Hayden, but I didn't see him anywhere.

But then, all of a sudden, I heard him. Yelling. It was faint at first; the stereo was thumping out some awful dance music, and the yelling was coming from upstairs, so all I could register was the sound of Hayden's voice. And man, was he pissed.

I moved closer to the staircase, debating whether to go up and find him. Then I heard more voices, voices I recognized. What was the bully trifecta doing here? I grabbed a random guy and asked if the football game had been canceled. "Other team forfeited," he said. "Those dudes have been upstairs for hours, and they are *wasted*."

Oh, no. No, no, no.

"It's not true! It can't be!" I heard Hayden yell.

"It's all right there," Ryan said. "Just look."

"I won't!" he yelled.

"You shouldn't have come here," Trevor said, and I realized he was talking not just to Hayden but to me—the whole trifecta was walking down the stairs, Hayden in front of them, Trevor's hand grasping the collar of his shirt.

"What's going on?" I asked, trying to sound brave, but I was terrified. Those dudes could kick my ass without even letting go of Hayden's shirt.

"None of your business," Ryan said.

Hayden made eye contact with me, and it looked as if he was going to cry. I didn't know what to do. Did he expect me to take those guys on? Ryan had been beating up on Hayden since they were kids, and despite his stockiness—he was short like Hayden but solid—he was the smallest of the three.

"Just go, both of you," Ryan said. "You don't belong here."

With that, Trevor tightened his grip on Hayden's shirt and lifted him into the air by his collar, which was already frayed. I could see it starting to rip. Ryan just stood there.

And then Trevor dropped him.

Which wouldn't have been such a big deal, except that a) they hadn't quite made it all the way down the staircase, and b) I was standing at the bottom. Hayden couldn't get his balance when he landed in between two steps, and he tumbled down the rest of them, his elbow hitting the side of my knee, which took me down with him. We both ended up in a tangle on the floor; I'd heard the crack of Hayden hitting his head on the wood and worried for a minute that he might be seriously hurt.

The room got really quiet; someone had turned off the music, and when I looked up I could see that everyone was watching us. At first people seemed shocked, though no one was exactly rushing to help. But by the time I'd stood up and figured out Hayden wasn't unconscious, the giggling had started. Just a few girls, initially; then some guys, and then it wasn't giggles anymore but full-on laughter.

I stopped. I wasn't ready to talk about the rest.

Astrid waited a moment after I'd finished talking before

she reached across the couch and put her hand on mine. I was so drained from talking about the party that I felt relieved—if she was touching my hand, if she was still here listening to me, then it meant she didn't think I was the worst person in the world. Even if I still thought so.

"What happened sucks, but it's not your fault," she said.

"Easy for you to say." What did she know, anyway? Nice of her to say it, but we both knew it wasn't true.

"You don't understand. I'm not just saying it, I know it." She was frowning, though it didn't seem like she was frowning at me.

"Oh, great, now you're going to be all cryptic, just like Hayden. You think you're going to make my guilt just magically go away?" I pulled away from her and stood up. I shouldn't have tried to explain it to her. What made me think she'd understand, anyway?

Just then I saw Eric, walking toward us. When did he even get here? "It's almost midnight," he said to Astrid. "We should get out of here." He looked over at me, all good-looking in his stupid skinny pants and perfectly arranged hair. "Hey, Sam, good to see you again. Need a ride home? I'm driving." And he was nice, too. I hated that I could totally get what she saw in him.

"Come with us, Sam," Astrid said. "It's been a long night."

"Thanks, but I'll walk," I said. "I could use some fresh air." I got up without saying anything else, as gracefully as

I could manage from that stupid saggy couch. Tomorrow I'd want to know what she meant when she said she was sure it wasn't my fault, but tonight I just needed to deal with the fact that I'd talked about the party, something I thought I'd never do, something I'd mostly refused to think about all week. And now I couldn't stop thinking about it, and I hadn't even told her the worst part. I needed to be alone. I waited for Astrid and Eric to leave, then headed for the door.

Damian caught me on the way out. "You hitting the road?" he asked.

I nodded.

"A little something for the ride?" He handed me a flask.

Sure, what the hell. Whatever was in it smelled wonderful, like rich caramel, and tasted like ass. My throat burned as it hit, and I could almost feel the booze reactivating the beer I'd drunk, making my head spin a little.

"You okay?" he asked.

"Doing great," I said. Guess I was a liar after all.

"See you around," he said.

The cold air hit me as I opened the front door; the temperature had dropped. It felt wonderful, though the shot had made me dizzy. How ironic, I thought, as I started walking, that after confirming just last week that I'd never be able to make friends at parties, I'd gone to a party and possibly made a friend. I'd been right all along, and I'd never be able to tell Hayden. It was almost funny. Actually, it was funny. I started laughing, then realized I was freezing. I looked down at my arms, covered with goose bumps. Which meant I could see my arms. Which meant I wasn't wearing my sweatshirt. Crap—I'd left it at the party, along with my wallet and cell phone. I had no idea what time it was, and I was getting dizzier and dizzier. I knew I should go back to the party, but I didn't think I'd make it. I was so, so tired. And I'd just reached the 7-Eleven, which had a bench right in front. I would only sit for a minute. Then I'd go back.

11

"THE MARINER'S REVENGE SONG"

THE DECEMBERISTS

THE HAND ON MY SHOULDER was gentle, but the voice was rough. "Get up, you stupid punk. This isn't your fucking bedroom." I opened my eyes. Standing right over me was a very angry man with a mustache and a 7-Eleven button-down shirt. His face was framed by the glowing pinks and oranges of a really amazing sunrise.

Sunrise?

Shit.

I stood up quickly and brushed the guy's arm off me. He must have been the morning-shift dude; that plus the sunrise meant it was probably around six a.m. Mom would be home at seven. I had to go. "Leave me alone," I said to the guy, and stood up. My whole body ached and I could hear my back crack as I straightened. As soon as I was fully awake I realized that a) I probably had a huge black eye from Trevor punching me, b) my head was killing me, and c) there was a better than fifty-fifty chance I was going to have to puke. Apparently I was having my first hangover.

"Don't come back," the 7-Eleven guy yelled as I went to get my stuff from the party.

Whatever, that guy would forget what I looked like after ten minutes, anyway. I wasn't worried about him; I was worried about whether I'd make it back to the house where the party was without throwing up. I also had to take a piss in the worst way. I'd heard that heavenly forces watched over drunks and stupid people, and since I felt like both I figured I probably had some luck coming. It arrived in the form of a cluster of bushes big enough to duck into, where I took care of both problems. I still felt like shit, but shit felt a whole lot better than where I'd started.

The party must have raged on well past curfew, because the door was cracked open when I got there and I could see people all crashed out in the living room. I crept in as quietly as I could and made my way upstairs to the room where I remembered leaving my stuff on the bed. Two people in semi-undress had fallen asleep on top of it, but I managed to get everything out from under them without waking them up, which seemed like some kind of miracle.

I practically crawled out the way I came and buried myself in my sweatshirt as soon as I got outside. My cell phone and wallet were still in my pockets, and I checked the time to make sure I still had some leeway before Mom got home. It was only 6:20, so I was fine. But seven text messages? That couldn't be right.

I scanned them as I walked home. They were all from Astrid.

Where are you? Text me back.

Every half hour, from three a.m. on. Same message, but I could almost feel the urgency increasing with every one she sent. Something bad must have happened. The time stamp of the last message was less than a half hour ago, so I took a shot.

You still up?

I wrote, once I'd made it into the house and up the stairs to my room.

Everything okay?

It wasn't even a minute before my phone rang.

"Where have you been?" Astrid said, whisper-yelling. She must have been at home.

I was too embarrassed to tell her I'd fallen asleep on a bench outside the 7-Eleven. "I crashed right after I got home from the party," I lied. Again. "Shut off the ringer on my phone. I just saw your texts when I got up to go to the bathroom."

"Thank God," she said.

"Why, what's going on?"

"You haven't checked Facebook yet, have you?"

"Nope. I haven't even gotten out of bed." That was true, except for how I'd just gotten in it. Also, she clearly hadn't yet figured out that I wasn't on Facebook. I didn't need hard evidence of how many friends I didn't have.

"Well, you're going to want to take a look at some point," Astrid said. "Someone beat the crap out of Trevor last night."

My stomach lurched. "What?"

"The cops found him in an alley this morning. He's got a concussion and two broken ribs. Looks like someone took a baseball bat to him." She sounded almost excited, but she was probably wired from being up all night.

"Is he going to be okay?" I'd wanted to see him get what was coming to him, but not like this. Just because he was a jerk didn't mean he needed to be pulverized.

"Yeah, he'll be fine, but he's done with sports for the year. Maybe even next year at college, too."

"I don't get it," I said. "We just saw him. Where were Jason and Ryan?"

"Nobody knows," she said. "Nobody really knows anything. Jason's still laying low after the whole Blue Star thing, and Ryan's parents apparently are such a mess that he hasn't left the house since, you know. Trevor was on his own last night. His parents freaked out when they woke up and realized he'd never come home, and they called the cops to look for him."

"I thought the police didn't get involved unless someone had been missing for, like, two days."

"Justice works differently on the east side of town," Astrid said. I noticed she didn't say "their side," or "our side" and it made me realize I had no idea where she lived. Now didn't seem like the time to ask, though.

"Did they find out who did it?" I asked.

She hesitated. "That's the thing," she said finally. "Trevor says someone clocked him on the back of the head and he doesn't remember anything after that. Never saw the guy. But some people on Facebook are saying . . ."

"What?"

I heard her take a deep breath. "People are saying it was you."

I started to feel dizzy. "Me? How?"

"Everyone saw you guys getting into it at the party, and they heard him threaten you. People think you went home, got a bat, and went after Trevor because you couldn't handle him without a weapon."

So much for making new friends. They all already thought I was some sort of vengeful maniac. "I would never do that," I said. "You know that, right? Please tell me you know that."

"Of course," she said. "I've just been trying to find you so you'd hear it from me and not someone who thought it might be you. And besides, from what Trevor said, this all happened after midnight, and I saw you leave the party way before that. I told people you went straight home."

"Right," I said. "Home." Now I had to feel guilty for lying, on top of everything else.

"I just wanted to make sure you were okay," she said. "I've got to crash now—I'm totally exhausted."

"Of course. Talk soon." I hung up the phone, and my stomach heaved. I hoped I didn't have to throw up again. The fact was, I had no idea where I'd been when Trevor had been attacked. I assumed I'd been passed out on the bench, since sitting down was the last thing I remembered before getting up; it only made sense that I'd spent the whole night sleeping there.

But what if I hadn't?

I'd never been as angry at anyone as I'd been at Trevor. At the party last night I'd wanted something bad to happen to him, and in some ways *I* wanted to be the bad thing. Who was to say I hadn't actually done it, in some sort of drunken blackout rage? Wasn't this why drinking was supposed to be such a terrible thing? Had I finally snapped and gone over the edge, like the loser in one of those songs on Hayden's mix?

Just then I heard the ping of my Gchat window opening up. I crawled back out of bed and over to the computer.

Archmage_Ged: Two down.

At first I had no idea what Archmage_Ged was talking about. I was so tired I could hardly focus, and I was still dizzy from all the booze. But then I remembered what he'd said after Rachel told me about Jason: *One down, two to go.*

Was he talking about the bully trifecta?

Except that left me with even more questions. To start, how did Archmage_Ged know the two attacks were related? And Archmage_Ged didn't just seem to know about the connection; he was all but taking credit for the attacks. But he wasn't real; he was either the ghost of my dead best friend or some sort of hallucination on my part, either of which meant I was nuts, but which also meant there was no way he could go around beating people up. The only thing I knew for sure was that I'd written off the idea that someone was just trying to screw with me. Not at this point.

I so wished my head weren't spinning; it would have been hard enough for me to puzzle through this if I were sober and well rested. But I had to try. Okay, so if Archmage_Ged was counting down, that meant Ryan was next. Normally I wouldn't think that was too big a deal. I wasn't all that broken up about Jason getting humiliated, although I didn't think outing someone was cool; I was pretty disturbed at the extent of Trevor's injuries, but I wasn't exactly weeping with despair that someone else seemed to hate him as much as I did. The thought of something bad happening to Ryan seemed almost fitting, given that I viewed him as the most responsible for

Hayden's death. Aside from me, of course.

But I'd told Mr. Beaumont that it wasn't my job to decide who should pay for Hayden's death, and I thought I meant it. The problem was, as far as I could tell, there were only two people who viewed the three of them as the source of most of our problems, and one of us was dead.

Was Archmage_Ged trying to tell me that I'd done it?

I didn't exactly have a good alibi for either event. I'd been on my computer Gchatting with the Archmage, who wasn't real, when Jason got hit, and as far as I knew I'd been passed out on a bench in front of the 7-Eleven last night. And I was covered in bruises—from Jason knocking me into the pew at the funeral, from Trevor punching me in the face, and who knew what else? Could I really be sure that all my aches and pains were from the things I remembered? Was it possible that I'd attacked Jason, or Trevor, or both? And that they'd fought back?

I couldn't picture it, and yet I supposed it was possible. More likely than Archmage_Ged doing it, that was for sure. I was so confused.

Once again I was going to have to go without sleep, because there was no way I could go back to bed now. My nerves were all jangly; I had to do something. Hayden's playlist was supposed to give me answers, so I pulled it up on my computer and looked over the songs again.

Hayden had included an epic from the Decemberists, my

all-time favorite band. I remembered the first time we'd gone to the mall together by ourselves. We were eleven and my mom dropped us off with clear instructions: two hours, no purchases over two dollars, no McDonald's. We broke the last two rules immediately, ordering five dollars' worth of totally random stuff from the McDonald's value menu and splitting everything, which was awesome but made us feel sick. We'd sat at the table and he'd listened to me bitch and moan about my dad, who had canceled yet another visit. He lived in California now and never invited me and Rachel out there—couldn't afford the tickets, he said. He would come to visit when he wanted to hit up his own parents for money, money they didn't have either, though I knew they always gave him something. Kind of sad when you get old enough to realize your dad's a d-bag.

"You're lucky you've got your mom," Hayden would say. "One good parent's better than two shitty ones."

He would know. He rarely invited me to his house, and at first I'd thought it was because he was embarrassed that his family had money when mine so clearly didn't. But after I'd been there a couple of times I figured out that it was really about his parents. His mom wasn't afraid to express her disappointment with him in front of me, and his dad was almost never around; when he was, he joined the party. His brother picked on him at school, and his parents picked on him at home. Even at that young an age, I must have started to understand that there was nowhere he felt safe except with me.

There was one other safe place, of course: the ITC. Our happy place. I'd never been allowed to buy comics—they were expensive and my parents thought I'd stop reading "real" books. Which turned out to be kind of accurate, though it still didn't mean they were right. Hayden, in contrast, already considered himself a collector. He made a point of buying the first issue of every new comic that came out, just in case one of them took off and the original turned out to be worth something. His parents, like Mom, didn't approve, but his father was a money guy and thought it was important for Hayden and Ryan to have allowances so they learned how to budget. I think maybe on some level he also respected that Hayden was thinking about his hobby in terms of investment, though he never actually said it out loud. God forbid he actually praise Hayden for something.

That was the day I discovered how into comics Hayden really was. I'd borrowed copies of all the old Batman series from the library, but he was into way different stuff. He introduced me to all the comics written by people from the bands we liked—there was one from the lead singer of My Chemical Romance, and one from the guy from the Dandy Warhols, even one from a bunch of members of the Dresden Dolls. I figured there had to be one from Colin Meloy, lead singer of the Decemberists. "He's all literary, and his wife's a graphic artist—there's no way he doesn't have a comic if all these other guys do."

This led to our first fight about music, the first of many, so many I couldn't count. I wish I'd realized how important those fights would be to me. Maybe I'd have realized how much fun they were.

I couldn't believe Hayden wasn't into the Decemberists—they were smart and creative and weird, all the things he loved. But maybe they were too smart; it pissed Hayden off when there were words in the songs he didn't know. I thought that was part of the fun, but he didn't see it that way. We were still yelling at each other right up until the time my mom showed up; I made her play all ten minutes of the live version of "The Mariner's Revenge Song" in the car on the way home, which finally shut us up. We sat quietly through the story of two men figuring out their shared history after being swallowed by a whale. "Sounds like klezmer music," Mom said, wrinkling her nose, but we ignored her. Hayden didn't even say good-bye to me when he got out of the car, just thanked my mom for the ride and gave me a little nod.

"Everything okay?" Mom asked. "You guys were kind of quiet back there. Did you have a good day?"

"The best," I said, and I meant it.

The fact that Hayden had put the song on his mix seemed in some ways like a peace offering to me. Unlike some of the other songs where we'd fought and the song he liked made it on the list, he'd picked the song that was from my favorite album, even though the Decemberists had eventually changed their style on the last album and made Hayden a fan. He could have picked one of those songs, and it still would have meant a lot to me, but the fact that he'd picked this one meant even more.

But it still wasn't my favorite of their songs. Which meant there had to be another reason he'd chosen it. It was, after all, a song about revenge; maybe it was that simple. Was it some kind of clue? Or an instruction? Had Hayden been directing me to take revenge on his behalf? Or could it be something even stranger? Archmage_Ged had manifested himself in my room; maybe it wasn't impossible that he could do it somewhere else. Crazy, sure, but not impossible.

But if Archmage_Ged was Hayden, I couldn't imagine it. The Hayden I knew would never have done something like that. Then again, the Hayden I knew wouldn't have killed himself, either. And I didn't think I was capable of hurting anyone, not like Jason and Trevor had been hurt, but Hayden had done something I couldn't see coming.

Who's to say that I couldn't, too?

12
"ADAM'S SONG"
BLINK 182

THE SOUND OF BUZZING WOKE ME up at nine thirty. At first I was confused and thought it was time for school; then I realized it was Saturday and I hadn't set an alarm or anything. Besides, my alarm was actually a dock for my iPod, so these days I was waking up to Hayden's playlist. It took a minute for my brain to de-fuzz enough to realize that the buzzing sound was the doorbell. Which was weird because really, no one ever came over here. Rachel's boyfriends usually just sat outside and lay on the horn, which Mom really hated, and Rachel never had friends over. When Hayden came over he'd knock, but of course it wasn't him. My heart jumped for a second at the thought that maybe Astrid had decided to drop by, but why would she do that? We'd just gotten off the phone a few hours before, and she must have crashed after; it seemed like she'd been up all night.

The buzzing sounded again, and I realized I should

probably get up and answer it. Mom usually went to bed right after work, so she was probably asleep, and Rachel never got off her butt to do anything, which left me. I hadn't bothered to change out of my clothes before getting in bed, so I ate a Tic-Tac to cover what must have been my disgusting post-party breath and ran out of my room.

Mom hadn't gone to bed yet, though, so she'd already answered the door by the time I hit the stairs. I couldn't see who it was right away; all I could see was a cardboard box, overflowing with stuff—T-shirts on top, who knew what else underneath. I could make out the design on one of the shirts—a mockup of the standard evolution series but with zombies—and I realized it had belonged to Hayden. Then I saw who was holding the box: Hayden's mom.

"Come on in, Mrs. Stevens," Mom said. It was funny—I'd almost never seen them in the same place together, and I hadn't realized how much taller Mom was than Mrs. Stevens, who was tiny. I wondered if that's what Hayden and I looked like standing next to each other.

It was pretty shocking to see Mrs. Stevens here. She'd never liked me, and she didn't approve of my friendship with Hayden. Mrs. Stevens was a slim, stylish woman, always perfectly made up, always with matching jewelry and handbags and shoes. Hayden had told me she'd been hoping for daughters, who she could teach how to dress and behave. Hayden's wardrobe of baggy pants and T-shirts had infuriated her.

She always said that if he wore nicer things, he'd have more friends. Great message. "Really, so she'd be less embarrassed of me," Hayden had said, and though he tried to sound casual, I knew it upset him. She kept thinking that if Hayden hung out with a classier crowd, like Ryan did, he'd be happier, more motivated to change into what she wanted him to be. She didn't know him at all. It annoyed her that he would come over here, where Mom would let us watch TV and play video games and he could eat whatever he wanted, though of course it was more from Mom's lack of cooking ability than a lack of respect for Mrs. Stevens's desire to see him skinnier.

She looked out of place here in a way Hayden never had. He'd always said he felt more at home in our house than he did in his own, which wasn't surprising, given his house. I'm sure it was architecturally significant in some way—it was super modern, all steel and glass and skylights, angular like Stephanie Caster's, like many of the houses in that neighborhood—but it was cold in every way possible. Stephanie's house at least had wood floors and some rugs to warm things up; in Hayden's house the floors were all tile and you couldn't wear shoes on them, and the temperature was always freezing. The few times I'd been there I'd worried about skidding on the slippery floor in my socks and landing on the corner of a coffee table. I figured the blood would be easy to clean up, at least.

Our house, while not even a little bit fancy, at least looked like people lived in it. Mom was a better decorator than she was a cook, and even if she'd found most of the furniture at secondhand stores, it was all comfortable. The chairs in the living room were beige and brown, and the boring shag carpeting was covered in colorful throw rugs that made the room look brighter, with matching throw pillows on the couch. I could totally understand why Hayden would rather be here. He had a favorite armchair, and we let him sit in it whenever he came over to watch TV, even though it was normally Mom's chair. There was even a particular blanket he liked, too.

I couldn't imagine Mrs. Stevens ever wrapping herself up in a blanket and getting cozy in our house, or her own. She looked like she even slept in a straight line. It was even stranger to see her carrying the box herself—I would have imagined she'd find someone to do it for her, though of course it wouldn't be Ryan. "Sam, why don't you help Mrs. Stevens with that?" Mom said.

I was happy to have something to do, so I took the box from her, taking care not to make any contact with her, physically. She was always so icy to me that I was afraid if I touched her I'd freeze.

Mom had no such fears, though. She put her hand on Mrs. Stevens's shoulder, apparently sensing that a hug would be going too far. "How are you holding up? I've been thinking a lot about you."

"I appreciate that," Mrs. Stevens said stiffly. "We're doing as well as can be expected, I suppose."

"I can't begin to imagine what you're going through," Mom said, "but if there's anything we can do, anything at all . . ."

"That's why I'm here, actually," Mrs. Stevens said. "We've started going through Hayden's things, and I put together a box of some things I thought Sam might like to have."

My first thought was that it was pretty callous of them to get rid of all evidence of Hayden, when he'd barely been gone two weeks. But my second thought was that it was really nice of Mrs. Stevens to think of me, given how much she'd always hated me. She must have been taking this harder than I imagined. I could see where it would be hard to have to look in Hayden's room every day and see all of his stuff there, as if he were coming back.

"Thank you, Mrs. Stevens," I said. "And I just wanted to say, I'm really sorry. I wish . . ." I didn't really know how to finish.

"Yes, I know," she said, but she didn't look at me.

I wondered if she somehow held me responsible for what happened to Hayden, if she blamed me. I would, if I were her. I did already.

"We were all so fond of Hayden," Mom said. "He was like a member of the family."

"I'm very aware of that," Mrs. Stevens said, and it was

clear from her tone that she didn't mean it in a good way. And without another word, she left.

Mom closed the door behind her. "She's quite a piece of work, that one," she said. "You did well, though. I'm sure she wasn't who you wanted to see right now."

"You've got that right," I said, shifting the box to rest it on my hip. It was getting a little heavy.

"I'll leave you to go through that in your room. And I trust you'll change out of last night's clothes and shower, at some point?"

Figured she'd notice. At least she hadn't said anything about my eye, though. I was sure I'd hear about it later. "I'll get right on it."

I brought the box upstairs and closed the door to my room. The T-shirts were spilling out of the box, so I took those out first—all of the ironic, vintage, and band shirts Hayden had collected. Even though he was short and round and I was tall and skinny, it all kind of evened out into us being basically the same size, and we'd traded shirts in the past. I wasn't sure I wanted to wear them yet, but I liked having them here. I looked at the wizard figurine, still on the shelf where I'd originally put it. It stared back at me. Guess I hadn't needed to buy my own keepsake after all, especially not one that might be making me hallucinate.

The rest of the box contained Hayden's gaming stuff—his Xbox and PlayStation, neither of which I had, his old

Dungeons & Dragons manuals—and a bunch of DVDs. All of the Star Wars movies, of course, new and remastered; all the Alien movies; the Joss Whedon shows he'd been obsessed with. I'd avoided all that stuff until *The Avengers* came out and turned out to be awesome. Hayden had tried not to gloat, but he'd made me promise to watch *Firefly* with him someday. Now I'd have to watch it by myself. Along with all seven seasons of *Buffy the Vampire Slayer.*

At the very bottom of the box was Hayden's laptop. The beautiful shiny new MacBook I'd been so jealous of. Why would Mrs. Stevens have given it to me? I could understand why she'd gotten rid of the games and the T-shirts; Ryan would never have been interested in that stuff. But the computer seemed somehow really personal, like something you wouldn't just give to anyone. I wondered if she'd wiped the hard drive first. Probably not; she didn't seem all that tech-savvy.

Worth taking a look, I figured, and booted it up. It made some noises that sounded vaguely familiar; I'd seen Hayden start up his computer before. And then, of course, came the log-in screen. Hayden's user name came up right away—HaydenStevens, his Gmail user name, nothing fancy there—but I still needed to fill in the password. I had no idea what it was.

I typed in a few things, halfheartedly—Radiohead, the name of his pet gerbil from when he was a kid, lyrics from songs I knew he liked. Then it came to me: it had to be Arch-mage_Ged. I typed it in, sure I'd nailed it.

Nothing.

Apparently it was only in the movies that you could just go in and figure out someone's password. Especially if you're a regular person like me and not some computer genius. I guessed Hayden would still be able to keep his secrets from me. Just like before.

13

"ALISON"

ELVIS COSTELLO

I SPENT THE REST OF THE WEEKEND alternating between trying to figure out Hayden's password and setting up his games on the downstairs TV, both of which conveniently kept my mind off the possibility that I'd somehow turned into a rogue revenge warrior without remembering it. I kept the computer on next to me as I played; every time I thought of something new I'd type it in, holding my breath in anticipation, but I wasn't having any luck. The games were a welcome distraction. Mom wasn't super thrilled about it, but I guess she figured it was better than Mage Warfare, since at least I was out of my room. Rachel was annoyed I'd taken over the TV until I told her I'd teach her how to play Halo.

"It's a first-person shooter game," I told her. "Not usually my favorite, but everyone seems to love it."

"It seems pretty dorky to me," she said, but I could tell she was interested.

"Here, hold the controller like this. The left stick moves your avatar, and you can use the right one to look around." I showed her how to do it and then set up a game where she and I could play against other people.

"How do I shoot stuff?" she asked.

I showed her the different weapons and we were good to go. It was fun to watch her get so into it; she liked the shoot-'em-up stuff better than I did. Except I couldn't get her to stay on mission.

"You get that we're playing as a team, right?"

Her avatar threw another grenade at mine, a quick-detonating one. In real life I'd have lost a leg, but maybe I'd still be alive. "Every man for himself, little brother," she said.

"You're not exactly a man," I said.

"Neither are you," she snapped back, and her avatar aimed his gun at me.

Time to bring this into the real world. I picked up one of the couch pillows and threw it at her controller. Or tried to, at least; I ended up hitting her in the elbow. It did the job, though, and her avatar missed his shot.

"Look, you actually did something useful," I pointed out. "Even if it was by accident." Her stray bullet had hit one of the enemy aliens.

But I'd started a war. I'd barely gotten the word "accident" out of my mouth before Rachel started pelting me with couch pillows. How had she grabbed them so fast? We started whaling on each other like we had when we were little, before Dad left, before Hayden, even. I took so many blows to the head my ears were ringing, though I'm pretty sure I got in a few good shots myself.

I don't know how long we were fighting before we collapsed on the floor, out of breath and starving. After raiding the kitchen for Mom's hidden stash of junk food, we settled back in to play another round. Cooperatively, this time, like we were supposed to in the first place.

We played for so long she ended up blowing off a date with Jimmy, which I would have felt bad about if we weren't actually having a good time. We'd trashed the living room, but it was totally worth it. I couldn't remember the last time we'd done something fun together.

I knew video games weren't going to solve my problems, though. They wouldn't help me make new friends, they wouldn't make Astrid decide she wanted to ditch Eric and hang out with me, and they wouldn't answer the question of who'd beat up Jason and Trevor, a question that in some ways I was afraid to learn the answer to. But they kept my mind off of everything, and right now, that was all I could possibly want. Sitting in front of the TV had the added benefit of keeping me away from my computer; I was afraid the Archmage would come back, and I wasn't quite ready to hear what he had to say.

But Monday had to come eventually, and with it came

a note in homeroom telling me to go see Mr. Beaumont as soon as I had a free period. This couldn't be good. I spent the morning ignoring my teachers in class and the stares of people in the hall who must have heard about Trevor and the rumors that I'd been involved. I could tell my teachers weren't sure if enough time had passed to start calling me out for not paying attention, but they all opted against it, for which I was only somewhat grateful. Getting yelled at would have taken me out of my own head, where I contemplated the odds of my having gotten so blackout drunk that I could have no memory of taking a baseball bat to Trevor. I didn't want to think about why Mr. Beaumont wanted to see me; I wasn't ready to deal with him yet.

I was still stewing over the likely scenarios at lunch, while I waited in line for a slice of pizza that looked as if it had been microwaved twice, listening to the playlist on my iPod on random. My appetite wasn't improved by the sight of Astrid sitting at my lunch table, waiting for me; the sight of her made my stomach drop, though in a good way. I took out my earbuds as soon as I saw her. She looked as pretty as ever; the streaks in her hair were different shades of green today, making her look almost like a sea creature and bringing out the green in her eyes. Her fingers drummed on the tray in front of her, and she jumped up as soon as I put my tray down.

"I know you don't really want that pizza, am I right?" she asked. Her eyes widened as she noticed my shiner, but thankfully she didn't say anything about it.

I looked down at it. The cheese was an abnormal yellow, as if someone had drawn it with a Magic Marker. "Not really," I admitted. "But it was the lesser of several evils."

"You haven't considered everything," she said. "Come on, you look like you need to get out of here."

She was right, but I'd never skipped school before. Kids in the college-prep classes I was taking never skipped school. And for all my online bravado I'd never done anything anyone would really consider bad, or at least I didn't think I had. But things were different now. Missing a few classes wouldn't kill me. "Where are we going?" I asked.

"I've got a plan. We just need to very, very casually wander out back." She pointed to the doors that led straight out to the soccer field. There was usually a teacher stationed in front of them, but I didn't see one now. "Mr. Cartwright's out and they didn't get a sub. He's the lunch monitor today. There'll never be an easier time for us to ditch. Let's go!"

"As long as you've got a plan," I said, but really, I didn't care. I'd have followed her anywhere, plan or not. I stayed right behind her as she walked—no, *strolled*—right out the back doors of the cafeteria, like it was no thing, even though she was carrying the enormous overstuffed bronze backpack she'd had at the party.

Astrid started laughing as soon as we made it outside. "You were perfect!" she said. "Didn't look back once. I was worried you'd go all Orpheus on me and turn around."

"Orpheus?"

"It's a Greek myth, where this guy's wife ended up in Hell and he could only have her back if he didn't look behind him as they left the underworld."

"I never read that one. But it sounds like the story of Lot's wife."

"What's that?" she asked.

"It's from the Bible," I said. "I learned about it in Hebrew school. God let Lot and his family leave Sodom and Gomorrah before he destroyed them, as long as they didn't look back. But his wife turned around and got turned into a pillar of salt. Almost the same thing."

"It's funny how much overlap there is between all the different kinds of myths and religions," she said. "I love all of it. I was obsessed with *Clash of the Titans* as a kid. I watched it whenever it came on cable. It really got me into Greek mythology."

"I love that movie!" I said. "The original, not the remake. I tried to get Hayden to watch it—I thought since we were both so into fantasy that he'd love it too. But he thought the Claymation was cheesy."

"It was," she said. "That's what made it so great!"

"I know," I said, though I felt guilty, almost as if I was choosing Astrid over Hayden. Though I reminded myself that I didn't really have a choice, not anymore.

The sky was bright blue and full of puffy clouds, not the kind that made me worry about rain but the pretty ones, the ones that seemed like they really could be made out of cotton. The brightness of the sun made it easy to see the path we were following, but occasionally there were low branches and weeds blocking us; Astrid would kick them out of the way so they didn't trip me up. She seemed to know where she was going, which was great, because I was completely lost. And I was starting to get hungry—I almost wished I'd eaten that radioactive-looking pizza. "Are we almost there?"

"Almost."

After we'd walked through the woods for about five more minutes I could see a field in front of us. It was a vast open space, with nothing but fields of corn and soybean as far ahead as I could see. In the middle of the field was a strange building that looked kind of like a barn. But not any barn I'd seen before—it wasn't round, exactly, but it wasn't square, either. Its wood was gray and faded; it didn't look like it had ever been painted before. "Is that it?" I asked.

She nodded.

"What is it?"

"An octagonal barn," she said. "It's one of the few left in Iowa. It's really old, and very cool."

Okay, that explained the shape. "What's so cool about it?"

"I'll show you." She grabbed my hand; her grip was firm, though her fingers felt almost delicate intertwined with mine.

I hoped my palms weren't all gross and damp. We started running together, across the field toward the barn. I could barely keep up with her, giant backpack and all; I was excited that we were holding hands, so it took me a minute to realize that if I didn't speed up I was going to wipe out, and that would be totally embarrassing. I wondered what Eric would think if he saw us and then put the idea out of my head.

We stopped running just before the barn. It was warm for October; I was a little sweaty, and the air smelled faintly of cinnamon, a smell I normally associated with spring—I think Mom had said it was from some native plant. The doors to the barn were enormous slabs of wood, with X-shaped planks across them. A latch held them together but Astrid just walked up and opened it; it wasn't even locked. She slid the doors apart and I could see the sunlight shining on the knotted wood floor. The barn was basically one big room that smelled like sawdust, with a rickety-looking staircase leading to a loft perched just under a very high ceiling. "You're not afraid of heights, are you?" Astrid asked, then led me upstairs.

Normally I wasn't, but the stairs were really narrow and creaked as we climbed them, and the floor of the loft didn't feel all that sturdy. I tried not to think of the prospect of it caving in and pitching us both to the ground, which I normally would, but somehow today I knew it wouldn't happen. There was something about what was happening that felt so perfect that I felt almost certain that nothing could screw it up.

Astrid dropped her backpack and opened it up. I'd assumed it was full of books, since it looked so heavy, but she pulled out a patchwork quilt and laid it on the ground, then motioned for me to sit. "This is more comfortable than just the floor," she said.

"No kidding." I was impressed that she'd come prepared. She'd really put a lot of thought into this. "Does no one ever use this place?"

"I think sometimes people rent it out for parties, but no one uses it as a barn anymore," she said. "It's kind of sad. When I was a kid, there were people my dad knew living in the farmhouse down the road, and we'd go over there and play with the animals. Me and my dad would come up here and look out the window at all the fields. Now I come here when I need to be alone, which has been a lot lately." She pointed, and I could see how sitting up here and gazing out at that expanse could be soothing, if you were sitting here with someone you liked, which I was. "We even carved our names into the wall—see? Still here."

She pointed. *Alison and Richard were here.*

"Alison?" I asked.

She nodded. "That's one of the reasons I brought you here. I wanted to explain."

I was glad I hadn't had to ask.

"Alison's my real name," she said. "Or it used to be. My

dad died last winter, in the middle of sophomore year."

"I'm sorry," I said, though it felt inadequate. I thought about the Elvis Costello song on the playlist. I hadn't given much thought to what it might have been doing there; now I wondered whether it meant that Hayden had known all along.

"Thanks," she said. "I know you of all people know that there's not much else you can really say. But I wasn't telling you so you'd feel sorry for me. I just wanted you to understand—he died really suddenly, in a car accident, and everything changed. I felt the loneliest I ever felt, and even though I had all these friends, and a boyfriend I'd been crazy about, it didn't matter—it was like they were all strangers to me. I knew I'd never be the same person again, and it seemed really important to me that everyone else understood that, too. So I started calling myself Astrid, and I changed my hair and started dressing how I'd always really wanted to dress and acting how I'd really wanted to act and hanging out with who I really wanted to hang out with, because I realized that everything I'd been doing up to that point was bullshit. My old friends kind of freaked out, especially when I quit cheerleading."

"Wait—you were a cheerleader?" I couldn't picture it. Then I looked at her more closely, tried to imagine her hair a different color, her wearing one of those stupid outfits with the short skirt and sneakers with pom-pom socks, and all of a sudden I realized I had seen her around at school before she'd changed, surrounded by all her old friends. "Right. I see it now."

"Too bad," she said, and laughed. "I was kind of enjoying the fact that you seemed to be the last person who knew. Yep, I was a cheerleader, and I hung out with all of those guys, until the proverbial shit hit the fan. But let's not talk about that now. Let's have lunch and not talk about anything that makes us sad. We've got plenty of time for that."

"Sounds good," I said, and it really did. I liked the idea that she was assuming we'd have more conversations, that we would eventually be able to talk about everything. And it made me feel better about not asking all the questions I had, even though I was getting more and more curious about her relationship with Hayden. Had he actually known her real name?

But right now, I was happy to focus on the food she was digging out of that backpack. Packets of sandwiches, apples, a huge bar of chocolate, and a bottle of water. She really had planned ahead, and the thought of it made me nervous and happy at the same time. So much so that I worried if I'd be able to eat, but as soon as I unwrapped a turkey and avocado sandwich, I knew I'd be fine.

"Slow down there, buddy," she said. "We've got all day. Here, have a drink." She opened the bottle of water and handed it to me. I supposed we were sharing it, which seemed kind of intimate, in a good way.

"I can't believe you did all of this." I didn't say "for me," but that was really what I meant.

"I've been wanting to get to know you for a while," she said, sounding almost shy, which didn't seem like her. "I wanted us to have a memorable afternoon, away from school and all the stuff that makes things hard."

I knew exactly what she meant, though it made me kind of sad to think about the ways in which things were hard for her. From the way she said it I could tell there were more hard things than what she'd already told me, but now wasn't the time to ask. "It's definitely memorable," I said. I wished I could think of the words to say it better, but being around her like this made me nervous, in a good way. I felt like I was hyperaware of every single thing about myself, and her—the way her sea-creature hair streaks somehow matched the vintage Celtics T-shirt I was wearing, as if we'd coordinated our outfits; the way a ray of sunlight coming through the window lit the spot on the floor where both of us were leaning on our hands, making her nail polish glitter and turning the hairs on my arm almost blond. I could hear that song playing in the back of my head.

We spent the afternoon working through the picnic she'd made. We talked a lot about our families; Astrid was an only child and was jealous that I had a sister, and nothing I said about pinching and tattling and practicing makeup on me would change her mind. "Come on, you're telling me that she introduced you to all the music you love and you're still mad about a little lipstick?"

"You can't ever tell anyone about that!" I said. "That's the kind of stuff you're supposed to do with your mom, but ours has to work all the time." I told her about my dad the d-bag, but I didn't get into too much detail—I didn't want her to think about hers again.

"Yeah, I used to do that kind of girly stuff with my mom," she said. "It's funny—we got along really well when my dad was alive, but now that he's gone, everything's completely different. She wasn't crazy about the new look, and now she's starting to think about meeting people and it's totally freaking me out. I mean, she's acting like we're friends, not like she's my parent, you know? I don't want to go shopping with her for date-night outfits."

"I get it," I said. "But don't you think it's better than her just assuming she's going to stay alone? My mom's been divorced for like eight years now, and I don't remember her going on a single date. She's just so stressed out working all the time I think she figures there's no point, but it's kind of sad. And your mom was married for way longer than mine, and nothing went wrong—maybe she just wants to remember what it was like to be with someone she loved."

"You're a much nicer person than I am," Astrid said. "Hayden always said that." She stopped and frowned. "Wait, we said we weren't going to talk about sad things, and here we are, talking about my problems with my mom, and now I'm bringing up Hayden. I'm sorry."

"Don't be," I said, but I didn't pick up the thread, and we sat quietly for a while. I loved being on the picnic with her, in a place that was special to her, and there was this moment when we'd finally eaten the last of the chocolate and were sharing the rest of the water when her face was so close to mine that I'd hardly have to move to kiss her. And it felt like maybe she was thinking the same thing, and maybe she even wanted me to. But another topic we hadn't covered was Eric; I wasn't sure if he was the boyfriend she'd talked about being so crazy about or the next guy on the list, but either way, I didn't want to be someone who moved in on someone else's girlfriend. If Astrid and I were going to get together, it had to start the right way, which meant she'd have to break up with him. But I was too nervous to ask her, and it wasn't just the nervousness of being around her; I was afraid of what she'd say.

We stayed in the barn until the sunlight shifted away from the window. It wasn't yet starting to get dark, but the sun was moving fast, and the sky was starting to fill with streaks of pink and orange. "We should head back," Astrid said, but it took a few minutes before either of us could bring ourselves to stand up.

I didn't want the day to end.

But eventually we cleaned up the trash from our picnic and folded the quilt together so it fit in her backpack. It felt almost like we were playing house. "Can I carry that for you?" I asked, trying to be, I don't know, gentlemanly or something.

She laughed, that great Astrid laugh. "I've got it," she said. "You just concentrate on keeping your balance in the woods."

She had a good point. With the sun starting to set it was getting harder to see the path, so I focused on not falling down. I tried to think of a way to ask her about Eric but I didn't want to ruin things.

"Why so quiet?" she asked, as we skirted a bunch of trees. Pine, maybe, from the smell. And the needles.

I didn't want to tell her what was really on my mind, so I had to think fast. "Hayden's mom brought me a bunch of his stuff this weekend," I said. "She even gave me his computer, but I can't get into it because it's password protected." I felt guilty using Hayden as a shield to keep from talking about Eric, but it's true that the computer was on my mind, along with a million other things.

Astrid turned around and narrowed her eyes at me.

"What? Do you think it's morbid and creepy that I want to look at his computer?" I asked, worried even as I said it that it might be true.

"Not at all. She gave it to you, so she wants you to be able to use it. You're curious about what's on there, right?"

"Of course." We'd finally made it out of the woods, and

the two late buses heading east and west were lined up in front of the school. "This one's me." I pointed to the west bus.

"I'm east," she said. Well, that answered that question. I'd spent the day hanging out with a cheerleader from the rich side of town. Never would have seen that one coming.

"I guess I'll see you later, then," I said. "Thanks for the picnic."

"No problem," she said, and then paused. "Hey, Sam?"

"What?"

"That password? Try 'Athena,'" she said, and then got on the bus.

14 "THIS IS HOW IT GOES"

AIMEE MANN

USER NAME: HAYDENSTEVENS
PASSWORD: ATHENA

And I was in. Simple as that. Or not so simple, really; I had a million questions. Who, or what, was Athena? Why was it important enough to be Hayden's password? And how did Astrid know? Not to mention the still-open question of what really happened to Jason and Trevor—my brain felt like a whirling blob of confusion. It was all too much. I had to focus on one thing at a time, and right now, I was focused on Hayden's computer.

I'd always been a little bit of a snoop. I'd found the hiding place for Hanukkah presents every year until I was ten, when Mom finally sat me down and said, "You know you're just ruining it for yourself, right?" Yup. I was just starting to get how much the surprise of the gift was part of the fun, sometimes even more so than the present itself. But even though I stopped looking for Hanukkah presents, I didn't stop looking through Rachel's stuff trying to find a journal (not a chance; she wasn't much of a writer, and even if she were, she'd be great at hiding it), or even through cabinets trying to find Mom's stash of Oreos (she thought if she hid them she wouldn't have to share, but she was wrong). And I considered myself the king of Internet stalking; the few times Hayden or I found a girl we liked I'd practically put together a dossier on her, though neither of us had ever had the guts to use it. At least as far as I knew.

This meant that the process of going through Hayden's computer should have been one of the most exciting things I could imagine. The combination of satisfying my innate nosiness and possibly finding out once and for all what had made Hayden do what he did, even if it meant confirming my own culpability—catnip, right?

Yet I sat there staring at Hayden's home screen for what felt like hours. I didn't know what to do first—check his email? Read his documents? Go through his music? All of the options felt wrong, and not just out-of-order wrong, but not-okay, bad-person wrong. Like many snoops I was a private person myself, and the idea of someone going through my computer, even after I was dead, was horrifying. It seemed like everyone these days was all about letting everything hang out, but not me. I liked seeing what everyone else was doing without revealing myself in the process. And as far as I knew, Hayden had always felt the same way. Looking at his stuff now felt like a major violation.

Not to mention that Archmage_Ged could apparently show up at any time, on the computer and in real life, and if he was really Hayden, he might be pissed. Maybe he was even watching me right now, crazy as it might seem. And if there was any chance that Archmage_Ged was somehow involved in what happened to Jason and Trevor . . . if he could make all those terrible things happen to them, what would he do to me?

But, I reminded myself, this computer technically was mine now. If anyone could look at Hayden's stuff without being overly judgmental, it was me. I really only had three options: 1) wipe the hard drive and start over; 2) leave Hayden's stuff where it was and just start using the computer myself, without looking at any of it; or 3) dive in. Was there really any question about what I would do?

I tried to be as methodical as I could. If it were my computer it would have been easy; I was a complete slob in real life, but my computer was perfectly organized, everything in files and folders with names that accurately described their contents. Hayden was the opposite, though—he was super tidy with his stuff, but his computer was chaos. He seemed to save everything to the desktop; it was wallpapered with files bearing titles that made no sense, or were misspelled.

Dyslexia or no dyslexia, this was the computer of someone who just didn't give a shit. I guess he figured no one would see it.

There should be a word for the thing that reactivates guilt, the trigger that made my skin prickle and my ears turn red, that made my head almost involuntarily droop, that made my pulse race with anxiety, then slow back down when I realized nothing had actually happened. Then maybe someone could find a drug to counteract it. Of course, there could already be one, but for now I'd have to manage without it.

I decided first to go through the documents. I reorganized the desktop so they were at least in alphabetical order, and then I started reading. All I found, though, were Hayden's old papers from school and the typed-up responses he'd saved from his teachers. The essays themselves were gibberish; he'd tried to write papers about movies or music he'd liked, but watching him try to explain the raining frogs scene from *Magnolia*, for example, was painful. Because I knew him, I could tell where he was trying to take really complicated ideas out of his head and get them across to his teachers, but their responses made it pretty clear that they weren't seeing it. *The number of grammatical errors is unacceptable for writing at this level*, they'd write. I saw draft after draft of each paper—he saved them all—where he tried to fix all the problems they identified. But his writing wasn't getting any clearer. *It doesn't matter how good your ideas are if you're incapable of getting them across to your readers.*

I'm sure they hadn't meant to be cruel, but I could imagine how he'd felt. Reading the comments, I wondered how close he might have been to flunking out, if they even did that anymore. I'd offered to help him a million times, but he'd always refused; I knew now he hadn't wanted me to see what he was doing on his own. He was one of the proudest people I knew, and look where it had gotten him. Based on what I was seeing, college was out of the question. Why hadn't his parents let him see a specialist? They were so insistent that no one know their kids weren't perfect; they'd expected him to just power through it on his own.

Next I checked his email. I anticipated it would be a gold mine; I went through all his messages looking for the word "Athena," but I found nothing. I did find some more confirmation that the school thing was becoming a problem; apparently he'd refused to discuss it with his parents, so they'd started sending him increasingly sternly worded emails telling him he needed to get his grades up. *Don't think that we'll continue to support you if you can't get into college,* his father had written. *If we don't see some improvement, you'll never get anywhere, and you'll be cut off. What kind of a job do you think you can get with grades like that?* Asshole.

What next? I logged in to his Gchat account and started going through the chat history. His cursor popped up: *Hayden-Stevens.* But when I clicked the list of people to chat with, the only person on it was me. I tried logging out and logging back in as Archmage_Ged, but though Google acknowledged that a user existed with that name, the account had a different password, and after a few halfhearted attempts, I gave up trying to figure out what it was.

I didn't know what to do now. It was starting to seem like Hayden's computer was going to tell me nothing more than the fact that his relationship with his parents was about as bad as I thought, and school was worse. Not exactly shocking, though. There had to be more. What was I missing?

Then it occurred to me. His clues to me had come from the playlist; he'd put it together to tell me something. Maybe the answers would be in his iTunes library.

Hayden's music collection was better organized than anything else on his laptop, though we had Apple to thank for that. I could see all the bands we liked, and a bunch of the ones I wasn't crazy about—Hayden had a thing for old metal and '80s hair bands, so there was lots of early AC/DC and Poison before Bret Michaels got hair extensions, a tour bus, and a gaggle of groupies with fake boobs to go on TV with him.

But there was also a category called "Angry/Sad Chix," which was filled with music I knew we'd definitely never listened to together, music I hadn't even realized he liked. Paramour, Evanescence, Skylar Grey—so that's where she came from!—Aimee Mann, even Alanis Morissette. We'd watched a video of hers where she walked around naked, and debated the multiple meanings of the word "ironic" and whether that made her song bogus, but that was as far as it went.

No, this list had to have come from somewhere else. Someone else.

I scanned the playlists, clicking on a few at random to see if they gave me any info. Finally, I found one called mix4anme. I wasn't sure what it meant, but it had some of the Angry/Sad Chix music on it, so it seemed like it was worth listening to.

I clicked on the playlist and cranked up the volume, just listening for a while. It was a pretty cheery mix, despite where some of the songs came from; the tone overall was definitely upbeat. Very not Hayden. In addition to the Angry/Sad Chix, there were songs from MGMT, Passion Pit, Metric. He wouldn't have come up with all of that on his own, I was pretty sure. It was music even I'd think about dancing to, and I hated dancing. This was the mix of someone who was very, very happy.

I tried to check the date he'd created it, but there didn't seem to be a way to find out; all I could see was the last day he'd played it, which was the day of the party. Had so much really changed in one day? Sure, the party had been awful, but could it really have been awful enough to counteract the happiness that had led to this mix? I'd thought I'd understood how the party had been enough to tip Hayden over the edge, but that was before I knew there had been this sort of counterbalance.

Which meant that whatever happened upstairs at the party was so much worse than I'd realized at the time.

I had to figure out what the name of the mix meant. I looked at it over and over again, sounding it out until it clicked. Mix4anme. Mix for A and Me. What if A was for Athena? What if Athena was a *person*? But who?

I looked at the Gchat window again, almost wishing the Archmage would come back. I'd pretend I believed he really was Hayden and ask some harder questions. I yawned and stretched, realizing I'd finally burned off the energy from the afternoon with Astrid, and looked at the clock. It was after midnight—it had happened again. I hadn't even noticed it was dark, let alone that I'd skipped dinner.

I'd just shut down Hayden's laptop and was about to pack it in and go to bed when the Gchat window on my computer beeped.

Time to play Mage Warfare, it said.

Archmage_Ged was back.

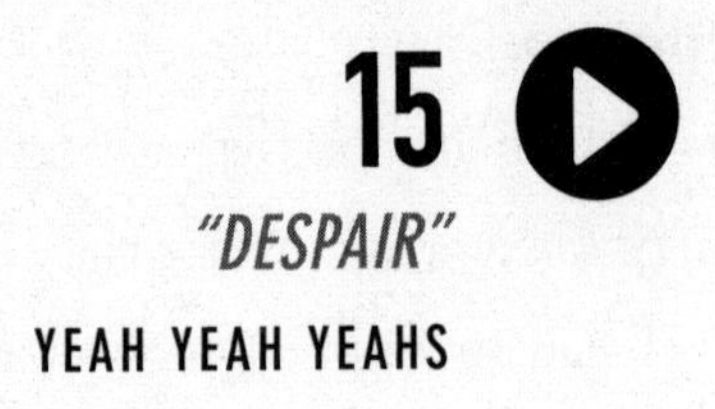

15

"DESPAIR"

YEAH YEAH YEAHS

I TRIED TYPING BACK.

Hayden, is that you? What's going on?

But Archmage_Ged was already gone. He was so annoyingly cryptic that I was starting to believe it really was Hayden's ghost. I looked around the room, for some sort of sign that this was really happening, that I was even awake. The wizard figurine sat silently on my bookshelf, like it always did. Staring at me. I felt a chill in the air and saw goose bumps on my arms again. Did I really have a choice?

Maybe Mage Warfare was a good idea; I could really use a few kills.

I clicked on the icon.

I played on my computer for a while, as myself, and while there was something satisfying about going in and kicking ass,

I didn't see the point, ultimately—why would Archmage_Ged have told me to play the game? And then, just when I was getting really irritated, my in-game chat window popped up.

Not here.

I heard the opening music of the game again, and I looked over at Hayden's computer. Somehow the music was coming from there, even though I'd already shut it down. It was impossible, but no more impossible than the other things that were happening. I opened the laptop, unsurprised to find that it had already powered on, that Mage Warfare was already loaded, with Hayden's character already logged in.

Okay, Archmage, I get it.

I played as Hayden for a while, just to see what would happen. I wandered through the woods in the game, finding a castle I usually ignored because the mission was to go in and save a bunch of serfs I normally didn't care about. But I was Archmage_Ged now, and it was my job to do things like that. It felt strange pretending to be him, and even stranger pretending to be him pretending to be someone else, especially since I felt an obligation to honor his playing strategy and fight for good, instead of just wreaking havoc like my character tended to do.

But it was getting me nowhere, and I was struggling to keep my eyes open. What was the point of all of this? Why wouldn't Archmage_Ged just let me sleep?

I could almost feel the Archmage getting sick of me being so dense. Surely there was a reason he'd not-so-subtly nudged me over to playing Hayden's game as Hayden on Hayden's computer. I had to be missing something basic.

Thankfully, before Archmage_Ged could make me feel like even more of an idiot by doing it himself, I figured it out. I clicked on the in-game chat window and waited. I wasn't sure what I was waiting for; maybe Archmage_Ged would tell me I'd done the right thing, or would give me a hint about what I was looking for. But five minutes went by, and then ten, and I looked at the clock again to see that it was almost three in the morning. I couldn't believe how the night had flown by, but my exhaustion had passed and now I was wired—there was no point in trying to sleep. I'd have to overdose on caffeine in the morning if I wanted to make it through school.

For now, though, it looked like I was on my own. Okay, Hayden, if you won't come to me, I'll find a way to you. I clicked on the chat logs. There were hours and hours of records of chats between me and Hayden, and a bunch of logs of chats with the random people we encountered in the game. Hayden was unfailingly polite to them, whereas I tended to get into online screaming matches with the strangers I encountered. But then, in addition to all the logs I was expecting to see, there were several files' worth of chats with someone else.

Someone named Athena.

So Hayden had another friend in the game, one I'd never known about, one significant enough that he'd used the name Athena as his password. I couldn't wait to find out more.

I decided to go back to the beginning. It had started last summer.

Archmage_Ged: How lovely to meet such a fair maiden.

Athena: And thou as well, good sir.

Nauseating, but not shocking. Hayden had this thing about being courtly to female characters, as if the game were some extension of the Arthurian legend and not the thinly veiled excuse for violence it really was. It was the only place where he was willing to take the risk of actually talking to girls. Most of the time it bit him in the ass—there were tons of dudes who created weak-looking female characters to trick saps like Hayden into letting their guard down so they could steal their weapons or beat them up in the most humiliating of ways. If Trevor had been in the game, that was probably what he would have done; my initial reaction was to think that Hayden was being set up.

Archmage_Ged: I see thou has accumulated much gold. Art thou as crafty as thou art beautiful?

Athena: I do not believe thou hast chosen the right adjective. Though I am but woman, I have studied the art of swordsmanship since I was a little girl. Every piece of gold I possess was hard fought. Athena is, after all, the goddess of war.

Archmage_Ged: Forgive me, my lady, for making such an unfair assumption. I can see thou possesseth great skill.

She'd let him off the hook for that minor misstep; his chivalry, for once, was being rewarded. And while her player history bore out her claims about being good with a sword, it also indicated that she might really be a girl: she spent a lot of her accumulated gold on jewels and armor that looked like dresses. And she was definitely playing the fair maiden in those early chats with Hayden. It was enough to make me gag a little, but clearly they thought it was super cute. They carried on for hours; it was the flirtiest I'd ever seen Hayden. Whoever this girl was, she really seemed to like him. I didn't yet know what role this Athena had played in Hayden's decision, but I was starting to suspect it might be a big one.

I kept reading. They finally dropped the Lancelot/Guinevere-speak and started sounding like normal people after the first chat session.

Archmage_Ged: I had a great time talking to you yesterday, but trying to remember all those "thous" and "dosts" was giving me a headache. Would it be okay if I was just myself today?
Athena: More than okay. I was starting to worry I'd have to find an Olde English dictionary. But you were doing a great job.
Archmage_Ged: Thanks! I'm not usually a words person. It was fun to think of it like a puzzle.
Athena: I know what you mean. I would have kept going, just to keep talking to you. This is better, though.

They were like this at first, flattering each other a little, both wanting to make it clear that there was something there but without having to say it too openly. That broke down pretty fast, though, and after a week or so of chatting they started getting real.

Archmage_Ged: Sometimes I worry that I'll always feel as alone as I do now.
Athena: Me too. But it makes me feel less alone to know that you feel the same way.

It was so fucking sad. I hadn't known Hayden thought that; we'd been around each other for such a long time that

I'd felt like it would be a betrayal to admit to him how lonely I was, even with him as my friend, and it turned out he'd felt the same way the whole time. It made me think I could have been helpful, if I'd just spoken up. Even as I discovered there were other reasons Hayden might have made his decision, it still seemed even more my fault.

Still, I needed to know the whole story. I kept going, and so did the chat transcripts.

Archmage_Ged: It's so weird that we've never met, and yet I feel like I really know you.

Athena: You do know me. You know me better than almost anyone.

Archmage_Ged: Do you really think so? Do you think it's possible for us to know each other as well as we think we do, even though we don't even know each other's real names?

Athena: If I tell you a secret, will you promise not to make fun of me?

Archmage_Ged: I would never do that. If you really know me, you have to know that.

Athena: I told my friend I had a boyfriend.

There was a pause in the transcript; I could only too easily imagine Hayden sitting in his room, completely freaking out, not knowing what to say. Finally:

Archmage_Ged: Not to sound like an idiot, but did you mean me?

Athena: LOL. Of course I meant you. Did that freak you out?

Archmage_Ged: No. It just made my day. My week. My year. You were serious?

Athena: As a heart attack.

Which meant that by the time school started, Hayden had his first girlfriend.

And he hadn't told me.

I didn't know what to think. My gut reaction was to be offended; we were best friends, and while he tended to be shy about revealing personal things—I'd always seen him as cryptic, but really, I knew how much of it was shyness—I had trouble imagining he'd hide something so significant from me.

But in some ways I could understand why. Because all I could think about was the possibility that Athena wasn't really who she said she was. The voice in the transcript seemed real, and she was saying all these really open and honest things to Hayden, so much so that I felt a little ashamed reading them, like I was eavesdropping on a private conversation. Which I basically was. But I couldn't help but think of that Catfish thing where people used the Internet to totally humiliate people who thought they were in love. I didn't think Ryan and his buddies were computer-savvy enough to trick Hayden in Mage Warfare, but that didn't mean there wasn't some other unscrupulous person out to scam him. Hayden knew me well enough to know that I'd at least ask the question, and I was sure it was a question he wasn't interested in discussing, let alone finding out the answer to, if there was any chance he wouldn't like what it was.

I was getting tired again; it was hard keeping my eyes focused, and I found myself reading and forgetting to scroll and reading the same thing again. But it was too late to go to bed; the sun was going to come up soon. And besides, I had to know the whole story.

I finally got up to go to the bathroom, then went downstairs for a Coke—I needed caffeine now if I was going to get through this. The house was quiet in the way only an empty house can be—Mom was at work, and Rachel had taken the opportunity to go stay at Jimmy's, though Mom would kill her if she found out. Every step I took seemed to echo off the walls. The old stairs creaked as I climbed them, which normally I could ignore, but tonight it kind of freaked me out. I kept expecting Archmage_Ged to show up in person again, which I knew was crazy, but it didn't stop my head from spinning around every time I heard a new noise.

Finally I took Hayden's laptop into bed with me and continued reading. The relationship between Archmage_Ged and Athena kept heating up; I'd gotten to the part where they talked about music, and I'd been right that a lot of the songs he'd put on the playlist came from her, like the one I was listening to now, a song that was a strange mix of desperately sad and optimistic. But things changed at the point where Hayden decided it was time for them to reveal their real names. Whereas Athena had always been open with him before, now she was withdrawing a little; I could see that this was going to be a real turning point for them. But I knew where Hayden was coming from. He wanted to know if this was real; he wanted more than an online relationship.

Archmage_Ged: I get that you probably live a million miles away, or are a hundred years old, or a dude, or whatever, but you can tell me. I'll get over it. I just want to know who you really are.
Athena: It's not like that.
Archmage_Ged: That's even better, then.
Athena: Not necessarily.
Archmage_Ged: I don't understand. We've already said that we know each other better than anyone else. I feel so close to you, but I need to know whether this is real.
Athena: It's more complicated than you realize.
Archmage_Ged: I'll uncomplicate it. Hi, I'm Hayden Stevens. I'm sixteen. I'm a sophomore at Libertyville High in Iowa. See, it's not so hard. And now you know

who I am. But if you don't tell me who you are, it's over.

There was a gap in the time stamps of the chat transcript. Athena was clearly thinking things over.

Athena: Fine. But I want to do it in person.
Archmage_Ged: Really? How?
Athena: All those things you just told me—I already knew.
Archmage_Ged: How?
Athena: I'm from Libertyville too.

There was another gap in the transcript while he processed what she'd just said. It probably completely freaked Hayden out.

Archmage_Ged: So we didn't meet randomly here.

He'd figured something out, anyway.

Athena: We had some help. I'll explain everything when we meet.
Archmage_Ged: Where? When?

I could tell he wanted her explanation to be a good one, one that was fitting of who he believed her to be.

Athena: There's a party next weekend at Stephanie Caster's house. We can meet there.

Archmage_Ged: If you really know who I am, you'll understand why that might not be the best place.

Athena: It wasn't my idea. That friend I told you about–she thinks it will work. There will be a ton of people there. No one will pay attention to us.

Archmage_Ged: Why can't we go somewhere and be alone?

Athena: Because I'm afraid.

Archmage_Ged: Of me? I promise, I'm not scary.

Athena: I'm not so good with people. And I'm afraid that when you meet me I won't be what you wanted me to be. I really want to talk to you in person, but I need to feel safe.

She was pretty self-aware; she knew herself well enough to know that being honest with someone at home in front of a computer screen was very different than dealing with them in real life.

But she'd given me one of the pieces of the puzzle: why we were at that party in the first place.

Who was Athena? Had she even showed up? How did she know how to find Hayden in the game?

My mind was racing again. I didn't know where to start figuring out the answers to all my questions. I finally looked away from the computer to realize that I could see the sun rising. It was almost time for school—I really had stayed up all night. The questions would have to wait. I closed my eyes. With the computer still sitting on my chest, I started to drift off. But right before I fell asleep, I came up with one more:

How did Astrid know about Athena?

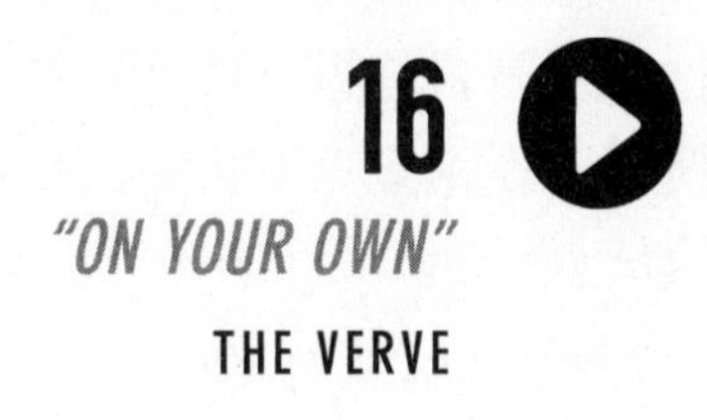

16

"ON YOUR OWN"

THE VERVE

"WHAT ARE YOU STILL DOING HOME?"

I opened my eyes to see sunlight streaming through my window and Hayden's laptop still sitting on my chest, though it had long since gone into power-save mode. My iPhone alarm had gone off but apparently I'd just slept through it; I could hear a song from the playlist in the background. Mom was standing in the doorway of my room, frowning at me. She must have just gotten home from work; she was wearing rumpled pink scrubs with little monkeys all over them.

"Overslept," I said, my voice cracking. I wasn't really awake yet. Not surprising, given that I must have fallen asleep at like five in the morning.

She sighed. "Get dressed quick. If I drive you we can get you there just in time for homeroom."

I felt bad; she looked as exhausted as I'd been feeling lately. I brushed my teeth, put on extra deodorant, and threw on my clothes as fast as I could. At least the black eye was starting to fade.

"Were you up playing Mage Warfare all night?" Mom asked, as I got in the car. "Or is something else going on? Were you thinking about Hayden?"

She'd pretty much covered it. "All of the above," I said, rubbing my eyes.

"Tell me what's happening." She ran her hands through her rumpled curls and I could see that she hadn't had time to brush her hair before herding me off to school. I felt bad for keeping her from going to bed; I knew how it felt.

I looked out the window as she drove, at the run-down houses in our neighborhood that gave way to downtown as we got closer to school. The leaves had long since turned, and the streets were littered with them, damp and crushed under people's feet and car tires. A few people had started putting up Halloween decorations; I turned away when I saw a fake gravestone with R.I.P. written on it in big, shaky letters. I wanted to tell her everything, but she'd just get worried, and she had enough to deal with. "I've just been thinking a lot," I said, instead. "About Hayden and everything. Do you believe something happens to people? After they die?"

"Like heaven? Harps and fluffy clouds?"

I'd been thinking more about ghosts, specifically ghosts shaped like wizards, but I didn't see any reason to mention that. "I guess."

"No, I don't really believe that," she said. "I think we need to focus on the lives we're living now. The dead live on in our memories. And our dreams. I dreamed a lot about my mother after she died, and I still do. Good dreams, and bad ones too. But I didn't mind even the bad ones. It made her still feel real to me."

Maybe that's what had happened. Maybe I'd fallen asleep sitting up, that time I thought I'd actually seen the Archmage. "How real? Like she's in the room with you?" I was holding my breath.

"Not literally," she said, pulling into the school parking lot. "But real enough that even now I sometimes wake up and forget she's gone. And sometimes I feel like she's watching us. Like she's seen you kids grow up, and she's happy. But that's just wishful thinking."

"Maybe not," I said, as I opened the car door. The air was cold and smelled like dead leaves.

Mom smiled. "You never know. Have a good day at school, okay? We can talk more later if you want."

I knew it wasn't going to be a good day at school, though, not after skipping out yesterday. I couldn't avoid Mr. Beaumont forever; my homeroom teacher gave me a stern look and said I needed to go see him right away. I braced myself and went straight to his office.

"Nice to see you again, Sam," Mr. Beaumont said, sitting in one of the big comfy chairs and indicating that I should sit in the other one. "Though I'd asked you to come yesterday. I didn't expect to have to come and get you."

"I know," I said. "I just didn't have a free period, that's all."

"I see," he said, though I knew that if he had a copy of my schedule, he already knew I was supposed to have a study hall yesterday afternoon. "Well, we can let that go for now. We've got lots to talk about today."

"Do we?" I wondered what he knew, what it made sense to tell him. For a moment I toyed with the idea of telling him about the Archmage, but the thought of saying the words out loud made me feel even crazier than I already did.

"We do, I'm afraid. I've been in meetings all morning talking to people about what happened to Trevor this weekend. Including the police."

My heart started pounding. "The police?"

"Yes, the police." Mr. Beaumont sounded stern, not at all the friendly, open confidant he'd portrayed himself to be at our last meeting. "From what I understand, there are two boys who've been injured at this school in the past week, and you've had altercations with both of them."

I felt my face start to get red. I hoped it didn't make me look guilty. Did that mean the police were looking into what happened to Jason, too? I thought he'd insisted on keeping the police out of it. That's what Rachel had said, anyway. I wondered who'd seen me arguing with the trifecta at the funeral.

"It's not like that" was all I could think of to say.

To my surprise, Mr. Beaumont nodded. I sank back in my chair, not realizing I'd been sitting ruler-straight. "I told the police I'd met with you, that I didn't think you were capable of that kind of violence," he said. "Now I need you to tell me that I did the right thing."

"Of course you did!" But I couldn't keep the note of doubt out of my voice.

"Let me tell you what I know, and then you can tell me what you know," he said. "I know that you and Jason exchanged words at Hayden's funeral, and then Jason was accosted by someone he didn't see. I know that you and Trevor got into a fight at a party this weekend, in front of a lot of people, I might add, and that night someone attacked Trevor, also from behind so he couldn't see who it was. I know that Jason and Trevor are Ryan Stevens's best friends, and the three of them, as you told me, treated Hayden very badly. And I know that you're angry and upset and missing your best friend, and we talked just last week about not lashing out. I believe it was a good talk, and I want to believe that you were listening to me, which is why I told the police what I did. But you have to understand how all of this looks."

Oh, I understood. I understood perfectly. I looked down at my jeans. There was a little tiny rip right at the knee; I pulled at a thread and it ripped through the fabric. It felt kind of satisfying.

"Sam, I need you to look at me and tell me you didn't do this."

I looked back up, remembering the conversation Astrid and I had had about lying. I didn't want to think of myself as a liar. I didn't know what to do. I had to tell him something. "I didn't do it." It wasn't completely a lie, since I didn't think I'd done it.

Mr. Beaumont looked at me. I remembered when he'd seemed to almost read my mind before; I wondered if he could read it now. "Why don't you tell me where you were when those boys were attacked? That will set my mind at ease, and then maybe I can talk to the police so you don't have to."

I felt relief wash over me for a minute, until I remembered that I didn't really have alibis for either night. But it was comforting to know that Mr. Beaumont was inclined to believe me, even if there was a good chance it wouldn't be for long.

"I was at that party Saturday night," I began. I told him how Trevor had showed up and started in on me, how I'd gotten really drunk for the first time and fallen asleep at the 7-Eleven. "I was really, really pissed off at him, but I swear I was totally passed out."

Mr. Beaumont frowned. "Did anyone see you at the 7-Eleven?"

"Just the guy who worked there. He woke me up in the morning." My face still felt hot, as if I were lying, but I wasn't. As far as I knew.

"Do you know what time you left the party?"

I shook my head. "I think it was before midnight because I wanted to make the curfew, but like I said, I was pretty drunk." It was embarrassing to have to admit that to him, but I didn't see what else I could do.

"What about the night Jason was hurt? Where were you then?" Mr. Beaumont looked almost hopeful. I could tell he didn't want it to be me. Not as much as I didn't, though.

"At home." It sounded lame even as I said it.

"Who was with you?"

"No one. Mom works nights most of the time, and my sister was out. I think."

"You think?" His eyebrows arched.

I sighed. "I haven't been getting much sleep since Hayden died. Everything's all kind of blurry. I don't remember whether Rachel was at home; I just remember that she's the one who told me Jason got beat up, the next day."

Mr. Beaumont leaned forward, elbow on his knee, chin in his hand. Like that statue of the guy thinking. "It's a little worrisome that you don't have anyone who can vouch for you either night. You may want to ask around, see if anyone saw you at the 7-Eleven, or talk to your sister about whether she remembers seeing you that night. I'll do what I can to help with the police, but you might still have to meet with them at some point."

"Does that mean you believe me?" I tried not to sound

too hopeful, but I couldn't really help it. If he believed me, then maybe I really was telling the truth.

He hesitated for just a second, and I knew I wasn't off the hook. "I want to," he said. "It just would be nice to have some verification. Have you given any thought to who else might be behind this?"

Setting aside Hayden and Astrid, it was all I'd thought about. But I hadn't been able to come up with anything. "They were all assholes. There must be someone else who had some kind of beef with them."

"You said 'all'—do you mean just Jason and Trevor?"

"I guess I was including Hayden's brother, too. Ryan. The third member of the bully trifecta."

Mr. Beaumont laughed. "Is that what people call them? Sorry, I know it's not funny. It's a clever name, though."

It made me feel better that he was laughing. If he thought I was guilty, would he do that? "Props for Hayden for that one—he came up with it. Far as I know it was just the two of us who called them that. I only knew about what they did to Hayden, though. I don't really know if they targeted anyone else the way they went after him."

"Hayden was a lot smarter than people gave him credit for, wasn't he?" he said, with that gentle tone of voice he sometimes had.

Nice that someone finally got it. "Way smarter."

"Ryan was the third, then. But only Jason and Trevor

were attacked," Mr. Beaumont noted.

"So far," I said, then wished I hadn't.

"What do you mean by that?"

"I swear, it wasn't me, and I'm not planning anything. I'm just saying that Ryan was the worst of the three. To Hayden, at least. If someone was going after Jason and Trevor, it only makes sense that they'd go after Ryan, too."

And I wasn't sure I wanted to do anything to stop it. Though if the police were after me, it looked like I'd have no choice.

17

"LET IT GO"

THE NEIGHBOURHOOD

I LEFT MR. BEAUMONT'S OFFICE feeling overwhelmed. It was all just too much—Hayden being gone, the Archmage, the trifecta. I needed to feel like I wasn't crazy, and these days, I only felt like that when I was with Astrid. I looked for her in the cafeteria at lunch but she wasn't there. Her friends were at their usual table, though, Eric included, so I figured, screw it—I'd ask and see if they knew where she was.

"Hey, Sam!" Damian, the bearded guy from the party, called out. "Are you coming to sit with us? Scoot over, Jess." He nudged a tiny pixie-haired girl I recognized from the party. She looked down but nodded and then moved for me.

I hadn't planned on sitting down, but what the hell—not like I had anywhere else to go. "Thanks," I said. I didn't have any food, either, but I wasn't hungry. "I was actually looking for Astrid—any of you guys seen her?"

Everyone turned to look at Eric, which made sense. He

nodded his head at me. "Sure, she was in class earlier. I think she skipped lunch to study for a test. I can show you where her locker is if you want to try to catch her before sixth period."

"That would be great," I said, though I felt kind of awkward. Sure, it was kind of weird that Astrid's boyfriend would help another guy who was clearly into her—I didn't kid myself that I was hiding it well—but it was cool of him to do it.

"No problem," he said. I wondered if he even saw me as a threat.

The cafeteria was on the bottom floor of the school, and of course Astrid's locker was on the very top, in the opposite corner. Once Eric told me where it was I wasn't surprised we hadn't run into each other much; the school was divided into four quadrants, and my locker was in the southwest corner, where all the lockers were red, while hers was in the northeast, with glaring yellow lockers. Just being in those halls made my head hurt.

"Sorry I barely saw you at the party," Eric said, as we headed up the stairs. He was wearing fancy pointy-toed shoes that clicked as he walked. Spats? What a hipster. "I heard you got into it with Trevor." What did he mean by that? Did he think I was the one who hurt him?

"Got into it?"

"You know, at the party. I missed all the action but people told me he punched you in the face. I heard you told him off pretty good, though."

"Yeah, well, he was always a jerk to Hayden," I said. "It was worth getting decked just to tell him what I really thought." I was almost afraid to ask, but I did it anyway. "Did you hear about what happened after?"

"Oh, I did." He gave me a sidelong look as we pushed through the throngs of kids rushing to their next class. "He kind of got what he deserved, didn't he? Like Jason." It reminded me of what Astrid had said about karma.

"Maybe." I wasn't sure what the look meant. Was he trying to get me to admit something? "Sounds like Trevor got hurt pretty bad, though."

"He'll heal," Eric said, trying to sound callous, but his voice cracked a little. I bet he thought things had gone too far, just like me. "Gives him some time to think about all the shitty stuff he's done to people, anyway."

"You think a meathead like him thinks about anything?"

Eric laughed. "Probably not. If he had any self-awareness he'd probably self-destruct."

Well, this sucked. I liked Eric. It made it a lot harder to hate him.

Eric stopped in front of a locker so covered in stickers it was impossible to tell what color it had been. It looked like an eight-year-old had attacked it—there were rainbows and unicorns and kittens everywhere. "She was not a fan of the yellow," Eric said.

"No kidding."

"Listen, I've got to run to class, so you're on your own from here. But we should hang out sometime. I know you're probably laying low with everything that happened to your friend, but if you feel like getting out, a bunch of us are going to my house tonight. Astrid too. You should come by."

"Thanks a lot," I said. "Maybe I will."

"Sounds like a plan." He gave me a fist-bump before heading down the hall. I didn't think I'd ever fist-bumped with anyone before, besides Jimmy. Was he being sincere in inviting me over, or was it just one of those keep-your-enemies-close kind of things, so he could watch out for Astrid? The funny thing was, I wasn't sure I cared. I liked the friends of hers I'd met so far, Eric included, and just the idea of hanging out with them made me feel a little less lonely.

Astrid didn't show up before the next period started, but I had study hall anyway so I figured I'd just hang out and wait, making sure to avoid the hall monitors. I put on my headphones and clicked a song from the playlist. It was from a new band we liked, whose music had a creepy edge to it that felt appropriate to me. But if Hayden had been trying to send messages through this playlist, I was worried I wasn't getting them. I had to pay more attention to the lyrics. This song gave me the sense that he felt like people had been lying to him. I may have done a lot of things wrong, but lying to Hayden wasn't one of them. I had to remember that finding out what really happened had to be my priority.

Astrid finally arrived at her locker just a few minutes after the bell rang, just in time for me to acknowledge that my priorities had shifted a bit in the last couple of weeks. I felt guilty even as I noticed that she looked as cute as ever; her streaks today were red, yellow, and green, and she was wearing a Bob Marley T-shirt.

"Sam!" she yelled, with a big smile on her face. "What are you doing here?"

I was so excited that she seemed happy to see me that I almost forgot to talk. "I was looking for you."

"And you've found me. But I have to run or I'll be late for class. Will you come meet me here after school? I'm craving french fries, and you promised you'd show me the best in town."

"I'd be happy to," I said, smiling back at her, so wide I worried my face would break. "See you this afternoon."

So much for my plan of taking a nap to catch up on some of the sleep I'd missed. But there were so many things I wanted to ask Astrid, ranging from the selfish (was Eric her boyfriend or not?) to the serious (how did she know about Athena? And who is she?). The afternoon seemed to last forever; thankfully I had English last period, and Mr. Rogers tended to ignore it when I fell asleep in class, even though my desk was right in front of his.

The brief catnap gave me enough energy to run through

the halls back to Astrid's locker as soon as the bell rang. She must have raced back too, because she'd beat me there. "I'm dying of curiosity," she said as I approached. "Where are we going?"

"Ever heard of a place called Peterson's?" Peterson's was an old soda fountain just outside of downtown, run by a couple who'd owned it since the '50s. They didn't have any kids, and a Coldstone Creamery had opened up a couple of blocks away, so I figured they were probably going to shut it down soon. I liked to give them business whenever I could; Hayden and I would go there after the mall sometimes. It was only about a fifteen-minute walk from school.

"Sounds familiar—I think I know the place you're talking about. It always looks closed, though."

"Half the time it is," I admitted. "They keep really weird hours. But they're usually open in the afternoon. Hayden and I used to go there after school sometimes, on our way to the mall."

She didn't say anything, just grabbed my hand and squeezed it for a minute, then let it go. I wished she hadn't. For the brief moment our hands were entwined, I had no questions. But as soon as she let go, they all came back.

We walked quietly at first, past the fields that had mostly been harvested, though a few still had tall stalks of corn for Halloween mazes. I could still pick up the scent of burning leaves. It felt nice to walk beside her without talking, feeling like it wasn't necessary to fill the space between us. Except that now I wasn't being honest with myself—part of the reason I wasn't talking was because I was afraid that the first thing I'd say was "How did you know about Athena?" There had to be a better way to lead into that conversation.

Astrid seemed a little jumpy, too, pulling at her extensions and almost skipping as we got close to the diner. It was almost like she knew that I needed to talk to her. Which I guessed made sense; the last thing she'd said to me was the password, and she had to know I'd have questions.

When we reached Peterson's Soda Fountain, I held the door open for Astrid to walk through. "How chivalrous," she said, and gave a little curtsy. Something about the way she said it reminded me of the chat logs between Hayden and Athena. I swallowed hard. How much did she know, anyway?

The soda fountain was literally not much more than that—there was a counter lined with peeling linoleum, flanked by stools covered in cracked red leather with bits of foam poking through. I knew it wasn't the most appetizing-looking joint, but I hoped Astrid would trust me, even as the thought crossed my mind that perhaps I couldn't trust her. "Here okay?" I asked, pointing to two of the less destroyed-looking stools.

"Sure. Where are the menus?"

"No need. Allow me."

"The gentleman is going to order for the lady?" she asked.

And I had that thought again—she sounded like Athena. Which reminded me that Astrid had said she was into Greek mythology. She'd have known that Athena was the goddess of war, like I'd seen in the chat logs.

What if she didn't just know about Athena? What if she *was* Athena?

She couldn't be. It didn't make sense; I couldn't picture Astrid and Hayden together at all. Or was it just that I didn't want it to be true?

I was saved from saying anything by Mr. Peterson finally making his way to the counter. He had to be in his nineties, white haired, liver spotted, and worn out. I used to try to chat with him; I wanted him to remember me between visits, to be one of those people who could get anyone to open up. I wanted to learn more about the Petersons than just the basics listed on the paper placemats he laid out in front of us, which gave the history of the fountain. But either I wasn't charming enough or Mr. Peterson just didn't give a shit—he never talked to me other than to take my order, and he never remembered me when I came back. "Know what you want?" he croaked.

"Two chocolate egg creams and a large basket of crinkle fries," I said.

"Egg cream?" Astrid asked as Mr. Peterson slowly walked away. "As in, raw egg? You sure about this one?"

"They haven't put real eggs in these things since the

1800s," I said. "It's just milk and syrup and fizzy water. But it's amazing."

The Petersons may have moved slowly, but they were an efficient unit. Mrs. Peterson was already working on the drinks by the time Mr. Peterson had the fries bubbling away. Astrid tried to chat with them while they worked, only to be ignored just as I always had been.

"I used to try too," I said, glad that she and I had the same instinct, but secretly relieved that she hadn't done any better than I had.

Mrs. Peterson placed the drinks in front of us, bendy straws poking out of the foam that sat at the top of the old-school fountain glass. Astrid took a long sip, eyes widening as she swallowed.

"Right?" I said, and she nodded.

"How did you even know to order this?" she asked. "I've never even heard of it."

"It's an old Brooklyn thing," I said. "I used to get them with my dad, when we lived back east."

"I'm not sure I knew that you didn't always live here," she said.

"No reason you would," I said. "I've been here since I was eight, but on the other side of town. And up until now I've never hung out with a cheerleader."

"A cheerleader no more," she said. "But I am a junior. Technically, I'm slumming, hanging out with a sophomore."

"I'd say you shouldn't let your friends see you, but Eric invited me to hang out with you guys tonight." I figured this was my opening. "Speaking of which . . ."

"Actually, there was something I'd been meaning to ask you," Astrid said, pulling on one of her hair extensions. "It's potentially embarrassing so I kind of want to get it out of the way."

Uh-oh. This couldn't be good.

"Embarrassing for me, I mean," she said, and I exhaled. "The thing is, we've hung out a few times now, and it's been really fun—I don't think I get along with anyone as well as I get along with you."

"Me too," I said, waiting for the "but."

"But"—to hear it out loud made my stomach drop—"you've had tons of opportunities to make a move, and yet nothing. Am I totally reading this situation wrong? See what I mean about embarrassing myself?" It was true; she was blushing furiously. Except that was not at all what I'd expected.

"You *wanted* me to make a move on you?" I finally managed to say, after metaphorically falling off my stool and picking myself up off the filthy linoleum floor.

Of course Mr. Peterson chose that moment to plunk a giant basket of fries right in between us. "Ketchup?"

"And pepper," Astrid said.

"You put pepper on your fries?"

"On the ketchup."

"You're a strange girl," I said. "But, you know. My question. You haven't answered it yet."

"The answer was implied," she said. "You haven't answered mine."

Good point. "But I'm confused," I said. "What about Eric?"

"Eric?" She looked confused. That was a good sign.

"I thought he was your boyfriend."

Apparently my timing was bad; Astrid had just put a heavily peppered french fry in her mouth, and she started laughing so hard she choked. Not quite Heimlich-level choking, but definitely potato-flying-everywhere, tears-pouring-from-eyes choking. I picked a chunk of potato off my shirt and waited for her to settle down.

"Oh, you sweet sheltered thing," she said. "You clearly have severely underdeveloped gaydar."

Gaydar? Gaydar! My new favorite word!

"Eric's my best friend. He used to have a very serious boyfriend, but that ended recently, which means he and I are both very, very unattached. I guess we do spend a lot of time together, so I could see where you might think—but no. Never. And I have to say, I'm extremely relieved there's a good explanation for all of this."

Double that for me. My heart started pounding so hard I could feel it behind my eyes. "So you're saying that if I made a move . . ."

"You'll never know unless you try, buddy." She was still smiling, and was I wrong or was she leaning in toward me?

So she hadn't been nervous because she was worried I'd ask about Athena. She was nervous because she was into me. I couldn't believe it. This was it, the moment I'd hoped for. I was so nervous my hand shook a little bit as I pulled a cheap paper napkin out of the dispenser on the counter, leaned in toward Astrid, and wiped a stray piece of ketchup-covered potato from her cheek. "That's better," I said, and then, finally, I kissed her.

18

"SAY SOMETHING"

A GREAT BIG WORLD

"WOW," I SAID, when we came up for air.

"Wow is right," Astrid said.

I kissed her again. Her lip ring felt cool against my lips, not nearly as weird as I'd imagined. Because I'd imagined this a lot, I realized, even more so than I'd been aware of. Kissing her felt entirely familiar, despite the fact that I'd never actually kissed a girl before.

I could have sat at Peterson's all day, eating fries, drinking egg creams, kissing Astrid, but I'd sought her out for a reason. Maybe there was something I was missing about the whole Athena thing, just like I'd misunderstood Astrid's relationship with Eric. I just didn't know where to start.

"So, the other day—" I started.

"When you should have kissed me and you didn't?" Astrid asked.

"No, not that," I said. "When we got back to school—"

"And you should have kissed me but you didn't?" She was teasing me; she thought I was flirting, and I hated to let her down.

"You're not going to let me live that down for a long time, are you?" I asked, although I worried that I was making too many assumptions about "a long time."

"Nope," she said, and kissed me again.

It was almost impossible for me to tear myself away. But I had to get my priorities straight. There were so many things I needed to figure out. I had no idea whether understanding Hayden's relationship and what had happened to it would help me figure out what was happening to the bullies, but if there was any chance of it, it could be the only thing that would save people from thinking it had been me. Myself included.

I pulled my face from hers, but I was still sitting close enough that our shoulders almost touched. I reached out and gently twisted one of her extensions in my fingers. "I always wanted to know what those felt like," I admitted.

"And now you know," she said, but it was like a screen fell over her face. She must have seen something in mine. "But that's not what you wanted to ask me."

"No, it isn't," I said.

She bit her lip, which was already a little red and swollen from all our kissing. "Go ahead. I'll tell you whatever you want to know."

I hoped so. "That day at school, when I told you about Hayden's computer. You were right. The password was Athena."

She nodded slightly. "I'm not surprised."

"And you never told me how you knew him. Hayden." I was holding my breath; I had no idea what she would say. I had no idea what I wanted her to say.

"Does it really matter?" she asked. "He's gone. None of this is going to bring him back."

"I know it won't," I said. "But I still have so many questions. I need to at least try to understand. If you know more than I do, you have to help me."

She sighed. "It's a long story," she said.

"I've got all day."

She paused, and then let out a long breath. I guess she'd been holding hers, too. "All right, here goes." She picked up a french fry and dipped it in the peppery ketchup; I could tell she was buying herself some time. I hoped it didn't mean she was going to lie to me. "Remember the other day, when I told you about that guy I was so into?"

I nodded. I'd assumed it was Eric, but now I knew I'd been wrong.

"It was Ryan Stevens."

I felt like I'd been punched in the stomach. A powerful surge of jealousy went through me, which didn't really make sense given that their relationship was over and hers and mine was just beginning. I reminded myself to listen, like Hayden had said.

"We met when I was a freshman. I'd just joined the cheerleading squad, and he'd just gotten moved up to varsity. It was so flattering to be hit on by a sophomore, and all my girlfriends thought he was so cute. I did, too. He really seemed to have his shit together, you know? He was smart, good-looking, athletic—everything I was supposed to want, right?" There was a bitter note in her voice. I wasn't sure what that was about. "I used to hang out at his house. That's where I met Hayden." Her voice softened again. "He was so sweet. At first he was shy, wouldn't talk to me much. But after a while he warmed up, and he'd let me come in his room."

"Where it looks like the Death Star threw up," I said, smiling at the idea of it.

She laughed. "Yeah, it was pretty geeky in there. And when he started talking about Mage Warfare . . ."

". . . you wondered how you could ever have thought he was shy."

"Exactly. Couldn't get him to shut up about it, but it was charming. I couldn't understand why he and Ryan didn't get along."

"The whole football-versus-geek thing didn't clue you in?"

"Oh, sure, there wasn't much common ground, externally. But you've met their parents; you know what they were like. Their standards were exacting, impossible to meet. Ryan tried as hard as he could and I knew it was killing him; Hayden just refused. Different strategies, same problem."

I'd never thought of it that way before.

"I did what I could to bring them together, but it never really worked. It didn't help that Ryan's friends were such assholes."

"Amen," I said.

"Anyway, that's how I got to know Hayden a little." She stopped, bit her lip again.

"What happened with you and Ryan?" I could tell she didn't really want to talk about it, but I had to know.

She looked down at the dirty linoleum floor. "We dated for about a year. Right up until . . ."

"The car accident," I said. No wonder she didn't want to talk about it.

"I was so lost after my dad died," she said. "He'd gone out for takeout, and I kept thinking that if I knew how to cook, or if I hadn't been hungry, or if I'd wanted pizza instead of Chinese . . . so many things I could have done to stop it. You know?"

"Yeah," I said. "I know." Oh, how I knew.

"And I get now that it's not my fault, or at least that it's no more my fault than anyone else's—the woman who hit him because her car was too old for antilock brakes, the weather gods for the freezing rain that made the roads so slick. But I was a mess, and I needed to get out of myself. That's where Astrid came from." She waved her hand from her head down to her feet.

"Astrid is wonderful," I said softly.

"Astrid is necessary," she said. "And I thought Ryan would understand. He had his perfect-kid persona to shield him from his parents; Hayden had Mage Warfare to get away. Astrid wasn't so different. But his friends, his horrible fucking friends . . . they made fun of him for going out with such a weirdo. My friends were no better; they didn't understand why I needed to change, and they got me kicked off the cheerleading squad for not meeting the dress code or some stupid thing. When Ryan finally broke up with me I felt like I had nothing."

"He broke your heart," I said.

She snorted. "Sounds so stupid, doesn't it? But yeah, I'd expected better from him. I thought he was different than Jason and Trevor, but it turns out I was wrong. And I'll never forgive him for it."

As happy as I was to hear that Ryan was well out of the picture, the way she talked about him made me nervous. I never wanted to hurt her like that, but there were still so many things I needed to know. Like the most pressing question of all: Who was Athena? Could she really be Astrid? How close had she and Hayden become?

"Look, I know there's a lot of stuff you want to know," she

said, "but this conversation is kind of bumming me out, and I was just starting to enjoy feeling happy. Can we maybe talk about the other stuff later?" She leaned over and kissed me again, and I knew my other questions would have to wait as long as she wanted.

"All right, kids, time to pay up." We were interrupted by Mr. Peterson. "We're closing shop." Was it my imagination, or was that grimace on his grizzled face a kind of smile? And what time was it, anyway? The clock said it was after six; apparently my loose grasp on the passage of time wasn't limited to when I was at home.

"Let's go to Eric's," Astrid said. "You should really hang out with those guys. And Eric's been rooting for you—he'll be psyched to know you finally made a move."

"No need to tell him you forced me into it," I said, and left some cash on the counter.

"You just needed a little prodding," she said.

Eric lived within walking distance of Peterson's, but in the opposite direction of my house, which made me wonder how I'd get home. "Don't worry, we'll figure something out," Astrid said, and we walked holding hands as if it was the most natural thing in the world.

I knew she didn't want to answer more questions, but I couldn't help myself—there had to be some innocuous stuff she'd tell me. "So, Hayden never mentioned that he knew you."

"Funny, he talked about you all the time," she said. "That's what made me want to meet you. The thought of someone as sweet as him and as cute as you . . ."

I blushed. She thought I was cute? "Did you tell him to watch *Donnie Darko*, too? He had that song on the playlist."

"The playlist?"

Even though we'd listened to one of the songs together, I realized I hadn't told her about it. "Yeah, Hayden made me a playlist. Before he died. There's a bunch of songs on there I know, and then a whole bunch I don't. He said if I listened I'd understand."

That screen fell over her face again. Maybe I had gone too far. "Yeah, I told him about it," she said, finally. "He thought it was too weird. He liked the soundtrack, though."

Now I had one piece of the puzzle. I wondered if she'd given him the other music, but I didn't want to push her away again. "It's a great song," I said. "What else is on the soundtrack?"

She looked relieved, and we talked about music and movies as we walked to Eric's house. Astrid, like me, was mostly into alternative stuff; we talked about how impossible it was to find anything good on the radio, which bands we liked. I paid close attention to see how many of them were on the playlist, but either she wasn't Athena or she was being careful—most of the bands she told me about were ones I already listened to, so there was no way to tell whether she'd given him the new stuff. I didn't know what to think. I didn't want her to be Athena, for reasons I wasn't sure I entirely understood, but I also didn't know what the alternative was.

"So, this playlist," she said. "Can I hear something else from it? Do you have your iPod?"

"Always," I said, and got it out of my pocket. I thought about what song to play for her. There were so many darkly beautiful songs on there, but they were so sad, and I didn't want to bring the mood back down. I wondered if I should make it a test—pick one of the songs I hadn't heard before and see if she knew it—but I wasn't sure what I wanted her to say. Finally I chose one, and we shared earbuds again, like we had the day of Hayden's funeral.

We walked and listened, the air growing cooler around us, the sun setting as we went, shades of red and pink and purple that seemed to make the cornfields glow. I hoped she was focusing on the part I wanted her to, about being the one if she wanted me to. I didn't want the song to end, but it did. It had to.

I stopped walking for a minute and pulled her close to me as the last notes played. We'd kissed, sure, but we hadn't hugged yet, and it felt so good to hold her so tightly, to feel her body line up with mine. She was almost as tall as I was, which seemed perfect just then.

"Has it helped?" she asked.

"Has what helped?"

"The playlist. Has it helped you understand?"

I thought about it for a minute. "Not yet," I admitted. "But I'm starting to see that maybe it wasn't all about me."

"That's a start," she said.

And for now, it would have to be enough.

19

"EVERYBODY KNOWS"

LEONARD COHEN

WE STARTED WALKING AGAIN and turned onto a dirt road with no name, just a number. "Eric lives here?" I asked, stupidly. I hadn't been sure what to expect from Eric, with his spats and his skinny pants, but I definitely hadn't called him living on a farm. Because there was no question that we were now on one. White house, red barn, sheep, pigs, chickens—it was all there.

"Not what you pictured?" Astrid laughed. "His family runs this place. All organic, self-sustaining, no genetically modified anything. They sell meat and produce at farmers' markets all over the state."

"So Eric is rebelling against all of this?"

"Not at all. He's super into it. He's got his own garden, and he sells his stuff at the markets with them when he can. He drives the tractor. Even knows how to fix it."

For some reason this was blowing my mind.

"You're not the only one who has another life outside of school," she said.

"Good point." She'd nailed it, but even more than that, I was embarrassed at all the many different assumptions I'd made about Eric that had turned out to be wrong. He wasn't Astrid's boyfriend; he wasn't some stereotypical hipster; the fact that he was gay didn't mean he didn't get along with his family.

Was I just as bad as everyone else? I hoped not.

From where we were standing, the farm looked idyllic. The sun had just about set, and the last faint hints of red lit up the white house. "Come on," Astrid said, and ran toward the door. Before I could catch up, before she even had a chance to knock, she was surrounded by a throng of children and dogs, all of whom seemed to know her. The kids all had varying shades of blond curly hair and were probably no older than eight; the dogs were a mix of yellow and chocolate Labs, as far as I could tell.

"Astrid's here!" the kids yelled, while the dogs took turns jumping on her legs and slobbering on her face. It didn't look all that pleasant, but she had this enormous grin on her face, which made me grateful I didn't have to rescue her. I am not a dog person.

"You came to play with us, right?" the oldest kid asked. I couldn't tell if it was a boy or a girl; all the kids were wearing jeans and sweatshirts and their curls were kind of long.

"Not this time, I'm afraid," Astrid said.

"You're always here for Eric!" another kid whined good-naturedly.

"Someday it will be just about us, I promise," Astrid said. "Now are you going to let us in or what?"

Almost as quickly as the crowd of dogs and kids had gathered, it disappeared, and the door opened. "He's in the attic," a voice called out. "As usual."

"That would be Eric's mom," Astrid said. She led me into the house and through an enormous open kitchen, where a woman in basically the same outfit as the kids was standing over a deep farm sink doing something that appeared to involve pulling the feathers off a chicken. I looked closer. Yep, that's what she was doing. "Hi, Mrs. Sueppel. This is my . . . this is Sam."

Was she about to say boyfriend? I hoped she was about to say boyfriend. "Nice to meet you, Sam," Mrs. Sueppel said. "I'd shake your hand but as you can see, I'm up to my elbows in chicken guts over here."

"No problem," I said.

"Okay if we just go upstairs?" Astrid asked.

"Go right ahead." Mrs. Sueppel turned back to the sink and continued plucking away.

"Was that one of the chickens from outside?" I whispered to Astrid as we headed up the stairs.

"Don't mess with Mrs. Sueppel," she whispered back, grinning.

The attic was up three flights of stairs. They were all wood, but it wasn't wood like at Stephanie's house or Hayden's, all even and polished and shiny; this was wood that someone had clearly cut from a tree by hand, sanded down, and nailed together to build this house, years and years ago. The stairs creaked so loudly as we walked on them I was worried I'd fall through, except that the wood seemed so solid under my feet.

"Coming through," Astrid called out as we neared the top of the stairs, which stretched toward what looked like the ceiling.

A trapdoor dropped down above us, allowing us to see a narrow ladder that first Astrid, then I climbed, leading into Eric's room. Except "room" wasn't quite the right word. His room was the attic, and the attic stretched the length of the entire house, narrowing at the sides where the roof came down. It wasn't like any teenager's room I'd seen before; it felt more like an art studio.

One side of the room was paint-spattered, with multiple easels where Eric and some of his friends were working. Damian was there, sitting in a corner with a sketchbook and a box of colored pencils. There was also a big plastic tub of clay sitting next to a wheel where Jess, the girl from the lunch table, was throwing a pot or something. She was the only one

I hadn't officially met; I tried to smile at her, but she looked at me quickly and then turned back to her pot, and I figured it wasn't a good time. I didn't want to interrupt her, especially since this whole making-new-friends thing was still not my area of expertise.

The other side of the room was filled with books and DVDs, and there was a decent-sized flat-screen TV hooked up to a Blu-Ray player and a stereo, though I didn't see any video games. Bummer.

"Hey, guys, glad you could make it," Eric said, coming out from behind one of the easels. "Sam, I take it you found Astrid okay?"

"I did," I said, and she grabbed my hand and squeezed it.

Eric's face broke out into a grin. "I see. It's about time, Sam."

I blushed again. This was all pretty new to me. "This is your room?" I asked.

"Mine all mine," he said. "Ran out of bedrooms when my little brother was born so I convinced them to give me the attic. I turned it into a combo art studio/movie house, so now we hang out here a lot."

"Your parents leave you alone?"

"More or less." He walked back over to the easel. "Make yourselves at home. You into art at all? We've got just about everything here you'd need."

"Not really," I said, though I wished I was. "What are you painting?"

Eric looked over at Astrid. Something passed between them that I didn't understand. She shrugged. "Come check it out," he said.

I walked over to the easel. He'd been working on what appeared to be a portrait of a boy, blond, with sad eyes. He looked familiar, though I couldn't place him right away. "You're really good," I said.

"Thanks. Can't seem to get it quite right, though." He frowned at it, then put his paints down. "How about we watch a movie? Everyone up for that?" He walked over to the rack of DVDs and scanned through them. "Theme today is teenage angst, just like every other day."

"You pick," Damian called out.

"Dealer's choice it is," Eric said. He loaded up a movie, and Jess and Damian started arranging stacks of pillows and blankets along the wall across from the TV. I guess they knew the drill. I found a big square pillow to lean on, and Astrid curled up next to me as a creepy song I recognized from Hayden's mix came over the speakers. Lying together watching a movie with Astrid was pretty much the greatest thing that had ever happened to me.

The movie itself was disturbing, though. It was old—from the '80s or '90s, I wasn't sure—about a loner kid with a pirate radio station. At one point he dealt with a suicidal kid who eventually killed himself. He felt really bad about it and ended up giving this long, ranting speech about why suicide wasn't the answer. I found myself fighting the urge to get up and walk out, even though the speech itself wasn't preachy or anything like that. It was just that I hadn't realized what the movie was about; even hearing the word "suicide" was kind of like getting kicked in the stomach. Hayden had never even tried to talk to anyone, let alone some random asshole on the radio. Would that have made things better or worse?

"You okay?" Astrid whispered as the credits rolled.

I nodded, but I wasn't sure I meant it.

"Not the most sensitive pick, Eric," she said.

He had the decency to look embarrassed. "I know, I'm really sorry," he said. "Totally didn't think it through before I put it in, and then it was too late, you know? No offense?"

"None taken." I didn't think he'd set out to make me feel bad.

"I was actually remembering the homophobia more than the suicide," he said. That had been part of the storyline too; I'd been so focused on the other stuff that I hadn't considered how the rest of it would affect other people. Like Eric. "No shortage of homophobes at Libertyville High, that's for sure."

"It's not as bad as it was back then, is it?" I asked. I couldn't imagine what it was like for him.

"It's better than it was, but it's still not great," he said.

"This is still a town where most people belong to one of two churches, and both of them preach the evils of homosexuality on a regular basis. There's no LGBTQ group at school, even though all the other big high schools in Iowa have them. Most people around here would rather stay closeted than run the risk of, I don't know, losing a scholarship because your church found out you were gay."

"But it seems like everyone accepts you," I said. "Your family, your friends."

"They do now," Astrid said.

"Let's not talk about that," Eric said.

"They'll get what's coming to them eventually," Jess said quietly. I think it was the first thing I'd ever heard her say.

"Maybe they already have," Damian said.

I wasn't sure what they were talking about, but I had a feeling it was Jason and Trevor. I didn't understand, though—Trevor I could totally believe as a homophobe, but I thought the rumor was that Jason was gay. I wondered whether Eric could have been talking about Jason and that church scholarship—everyone knew how religious his family was, and he was definitely the type to win scholarship money.

The room was quiet after that, but it wasn't a normal silence. It was filled with something—I couldn't tell exactly what, but something wasn't right. Did they all think I'd done it, too? I wanted to say that I hadn't, that it must have been someone else, but I couldn't be sure, and I didn't want to lie.

"It's getting late," someone said. "We should probably head out."

"Yeah, we should too," Astrid said. "Can anyone give us a ride?"

Damian had borrowed his dad's car, so he offered to drop us off. I thought maybe I'd get to see where Astrid lived, but Damian went by my house first. "Good to see you guys," he said. "We should all hang out again soon."

"If I don't keep Sam all to myself," Astrid said. She kissed me before I got out of the car.

If she kept kissing me like that, I imagined, maybe the other stuff wouldn't matter so much. But I felt guilty even thinking it.

20

"HOW TO FIGHT LONELINESS"

WILCO

MOM, RACHEL, AND JIMMY were all hanging out in the living room when I got home. "Did I miss a party?" I asked. There was an empty box of pizza on the coffee table. "Is this becoming a weekly thing?"

Mom lounged in her usual chair, the one that Hayden had always liked. "Did you meet with the guidance counselor? The school called, you know."

"Forget the guidance counselor," Rachel said. "I heard you've been hanging around with Alison Whitman."

Word traveled fast. "She goes by Astrid now."

"Is that the girl who came over before that party?" Mom asked. "She has an . . . unusual sense of style."

Rachel snorted. "Weird, you mean."

"You're one to talk," I pointed out. Rachel's current ensemble included yet another tiny skirt, plus eye shadow in so many shades of pink, purple, and orange that her eyes looked like the sunset I'd just seen.

"Peace, all," Jimmy said, which was also hilarious since he appeared to be wearing some sort of studded dog collar. He didn't exactly look like the U.N. But it seemed to work, or at least it bought me a minute to drop my stuff and sit down on the couch.

"What did you and the guidance counselor talk about?" Mom asked.

I glanced over at Jimmy. "Glad to know we've got such a good sense of boundaries around here," I said. "Beaumont said it was confidential."

"Nice try," Mom said. "Nothing's confidential from your mother."

Yeah, I hadn't expected that to work. "We talked mostly about Hayden. And some weird stuff that's been happening at school."

"Like Trevor Floyd getting beat up after that party you went to?" Rachel asked. "It's all anyone's talking about. You know what the rumors are, right?"

"Yeah, I know."

"What rumors?" Mom asked. "I know I'm not around as much as I'd like, but that means you kids need to do a better job of keeping me informed."

Rachel laughed. "Relax, Mom. The rumor is that Chickenbutt over here is responsible, but look at him. There's no way he could beat up a guy that big."

"Piss off, Rachel," I said.

"Language, Sam!" Mom gave me a stern look.

Rachel had called me Chickenbutt since I was little, because I'd always been so scrawny. It was true I hadn't filled out much, if at all, but it was kind of offensive that she didn't think I was capable of doing something. Making an impact. I mean, I wanted it to not be true, but still.

"You'd be surprised what people can do when they're pushed," Jimmy said. "Not that I'm saying you did anything, Sam. Just saying."

I knew what he meant, and I felt oddly grateful to him for saying it.

"Sam, you came right home from the party, didn't you?" Mom asked, brow furrowed.

"Of course, Mom." Even though I was getting more and more worried about that all the time, there was no need to give her something else to worry about. "So are there any other theories about who might have done this?" I asked Rachel. "Besides me?"

"Well, some people think they aren't connected," she said. "People kind of knew about Jason already. And you know Trevor. He's always been a—" She looked over at Mom. "—a very not nice person."

"Could have been his 'roid dealer," I said.

"I think people usually get steroids from their gyms," Jimmy said. Mom gave him a "you-would-know" look, and

Jimmy held his hands up. "No personal knowledge here. Just city living."

"Do you miss it there?" I asked. Anything to change the subject.

"Yeah, I do," he said. "But I'm hoping to head back there for college."

Mom's eyes widened. "College?" she asked hopefully. "For some reason I assumed you weren't in high school now."

"Because I look like a dropout?" He laughed. "I had enough credits to graduate a year early, between my AP classes and some college courses I'd been taking on the side. They gave me a diploma before I left. I'm spending the year taking some online science classes and working on nailing the SAT so I can get a scholarship. I'm going to be a doctor."

He said it with confidence—not "I want to be a doctor," or "I'm hoping to be a doctor," but "I'm going to be." And I believed him.

"See?" Rachel said. "Don't judge a book by its cover, Mom."

"Guilty as charged," she said.

Apparently I wasn't the only one who was finding people surprising these days. It made me wonder whether everyone had these secret lives, these aspects of themselves that didn't match who they seemed to be. Just thinking about it made me tired, though, and I remembered that I'd all but pulled an all-nighter the night before. I had to make up some ground. I was just about to make my excuses when Jimmy said, "Sam, you got a minute?"

"Sure," I said, though I had no idea what he wanted. "I was just about to go upstairs and try to crash early. Mind if we hang out in my room?"

I saw him look over at Rachel, and she gave a little nod. So they'd planned this.

We went upstairs; I sat on my bed while Jimmy looked around at all my stuff. "Nice book collection," he said. "You a big reader?"

"Used to be," I said. "I'm more into video games now."

He smiled. "Rachel mentioned that. You know she blew me off when you guys were playing Halo, right?"

"Yeah, sorry about that," I said. "I wasn't expecting it."

"Me neither," he said. "But I was glad you guys were bonding."

Who was this guy? "I don't know if I'd call it that."

"Well, you should know that she's looking out for you," he said. "And I just wanted to say that I know we don't know each other that well, but there aren't that many people in the world who've gone through the stuff we have. I just wanted to see how you were doing."

"I've been better," I admitted. There were actually a lot of things I wanted to ask him, like whether he'd had anything weird happen to him, like whether he'd seen his friend even after he was gone, but I couldn't find the words to say it without sounding like an insane person. But there was one thing. "When did it get better?" I asked. "When did you start to feel like it was okay to, like, be in the world again?" I didn't know how to describe the mixture of elation and guilt I was feeling about Astrid, so I didn't try.

"That's a tough one," he said, and sat down on the bed with me. "It wasn't an all-of-a-sudden kind of thing. I think I just went through the motions for a while—I tried being normal, going to school and all that, but it wasn't working for me. I guess I wanted closure, but I was never going to get it, because the only person who could tell me why things had gone down the way they did was dead. Once I made my peace with that, I started being able to think about other things. Moving helped, too—I needed some distance. Does that help at all?"

"A little," I said, which was accurate. I didn't have the option of moving, and while I got what he was saying about closure, Hayden had kind of left the door open—he'd all but told me that there was something to figure out, so I needed to do it.

"I know it's not the same for you," he said. "But maybe it will help to keep busy, do new things. Rachel mentioned that there was a girl . . ."

"I don't want to talk—"

He held up his hands. "I'm not asking. I'm just saying you should go with it. You won't be able to stop thinking about what happened if you sit home by yourself. Listen, Rachel was telling me about this thing happening over the weekend she thought I'd get a kick out of—something called mudding? Whatever it is, we don't have it in Chicago. You should come with us."

I'd heard of it—it sounded kind of stupid. Guys in trucks basically drag racing in the mud. Kind of a macho thing. Trevor used to race in his enormous red pickup sometimes, but apparently he wasn't very good at it. Didn't seem like something I'd be into, but Rachel's boyfriends had always been into it, and she must have liked it, too, because she always went with them. "I don't know," I said.

Rachel came down the hall and stood in the doorway, as if on cue. I wondered if she'd been eavesdropping. Wouldn't be the first time. "Come on, it'll be something different," she said. She actually wanted me to go? With her, in public? This was new. "It's one of the few social events at school where anyone can go and not feel weird. People don't get all judgy. They just get dirty."

"I'll consider it," I said.

"Think of it as a favor to me," Jimmy said. "I don't think I'll be in my element there, you know?"

Oh, I did.

Once he left, I debated whether to turn on the computer or just go straight to bed. But there was so much swirling around in my head and I just wished there was someone I could talk to about it. The problem was, the person I really wanted to talk to was Hayden. When would I stop feeling this way? When would he stop being the first person I wanted to call whenever anything happened?

Maybe it was time to give in. Even if I was delusional, there was a good chance I could turn on my computer right now and someone named Archmage_Ged would show up. And maybe he'd be cryptic and annoying, just like Hayden, but maybe he would also listen. Like he'd asked me to do.

It was worth a shot. I booted up the computer and logged into Gchat.

Sam_Goldsmith: Are you here?

And then I inhaled deeply, and wrote:

I believe you now.

It wasn't entirely true, but it didn't matter.

The cursor blinked for a long time, so long I thought maybe I'd fallen asleep when I heard the ping of a new message.

Archmage_Ged: Really?

I could almost feel hopefulness in the word. It sounded like Hayden.

Sam_Goldsmith: Sure.

I couldn't help but sound skeptical. I was never very good at lying to him.

Archmage_Ged: Do you need someone to talk to? Is that it?
Sam_Goldsmith: Kind of. I've been listening to the playlist and I'm trying to figure things out, but I need help.

That was the truth, for sure.

Archmage_Ged: I'm afraid there's not much I can do, not from here.
Sam_Goldsmith: Where's "here"?

This was getting interesting.

Archmage_Ged: Are you trying to start a conversation about the afterlife? I don't think that's a good idea.

If this was Hayden, he was as maddening as ever.

Sam_Goldsmith: Can't you tell me something?

Anything? Who's Athena? What happened to Jason and Trevor? Tell me I'm not crazy.
Archmage_Ged: I can't tell you that. You were always batshit.

I almost started laughing, but I was too frustrated.

Sam_Goldsmith: Come on, give me something.
Archmage_Ged: What is it that you really need to know that you don't know already, that matters? Jason and Trevor are assholes who got what they deserve. Athena was a secret I kept from you, and I know that makes you mad, but wasn't I allowed to have secrets?

Not from me, I wanted to write.

Sam_Goldsmith: Just tell me. Who hurt Jason and Trevor? Was it you? Was it me?
Archmage_Ged: Like I said, does it really matter?

Was he kidding? Did he not see how much it mattered?

Sam_Goldsmith: It does to me. I could be in real trouble here.
Archmage_Ged: You'll be fine.

I wondered if he was just telling me what I wanted to hear.

Archmage_Ged: You have Astrid now, right?

How did he know that?

Sam_Goldsmith: I think so. I hope so. But I still have so many questions. Anything you want to tell me? Secrets you want to share?

Archmage_Ged: You're mad I didn't tell you about her before. I understand.

Of course he did. He always understood. I shivered a little, even though it wasn't cold.

Archmage_Ged: I wanted you to meet her someday. I knew you'd be good for each other.

Sam_Goldsmith: Were we supposed to share her or something?

I wasn't completely convinced that she was Athena; there were so many things about it that didn't make sense. But right now it was the only option I had. And I hadn't even begun to deal with the idea of me and Hayden being into the same girl.

The cursor blinked. Was he not going to explain?

Sam_Goldsmith: Hello?

The cursor blinked again. I heard thunder outside my window, and then the crack and flash of a bolt of lightning. It started to rain, slowly at first, then in loud, pounding drops that clattered on the roof so hard I wondered if it might be hailing, too. After what felt like at least fifteen minutes I looked at the clock, only to once again be surprised to find how many hours had passed.

Finally, the Archmage started typing again.

Archmage_Ged: The answers are all in the playlist.
Time for act three.

And then he was gone.

21

"CONVERSATION 16"

THE NATIONAL

I'D HAD ENOUGH OF ARCHMAGE_GED and his cryptic bullshit. Between him showing up and me goading him into showing up I was never going to sleep again. And if I stayed as fuzzy as I had been, who knew what would happen? "Time for act three"?

That had to mean Ryan was next.

I didn't know what to do. The more I learned, the more I hated him. He'd been a terrible brother to Hayden, and it turned out he'd been a terrible boyfriend to Astrid, too. Why should I care if something bad happened to him?

But I wasn't a big fan of Jason or Trevor, either, and I still felt sick inside thinking about what had happened to them. Sure, they deserved it, to a point, but not like that. Part of the reason I hated to think that I might be responsible was because things hadn't gone down the way I would have wanted them to. I didn't like all these secrets; I wanted things out in the open. I wanted the world to know that all three of those guys were bad people; having bad things happen to them wasn't the same with making them, and everyone else, deal with who they really were.

I realized, then, that I didn't want something mysterious and bad to happen to Ryan. I wanted him to have to face who he was and how that made him responsible. Which meant I had to stop whatever was supposed to happen next.

But first I had to figure out what that was.

I fell asleep listening to the playlist, hoping some clue was buried in the lyrics, but I wasn't getting it. More songs about sadness, about love, about death . . . I didn't know what to do except try and figure out where some of them had come from. That meant I had to find out, once and for all, whether Athena was really Astrid. And I knew where I had to start.

I texted Astrid to see if she could meet me after school; I knew we didn't share a lunch period that day. And then I picked the most soothing song on the playlist and got some much-needed sleep.

I spent the day at school alternating between trying to figure out what exactly to say to her and how to avoid the stares and whispers of the other students, who obviously had all heard the rumors about Jason and Trevor. Every time I heard footsteps behind me in the halls I flinched, sure that the police had finally decided to question me. It was only a matter of time.

The plan was to meet up at the mall. I went there straight

from school; I had last period off, and I wanted some time to hang out at the ITC. I hadn't been there since the day of Hayden's funeral, and I was used to going there all the time. I hoped the manager wouldn't ask me about Hayden again, but I could handle it. Besides, the new *American Vampire* was out, and I'd been making a point of reading it in the store when I could get away with it so I wouldn't have to buy the hardcovers. Stephen King had written the first one, and he was one of my favorite writers—I'd read all his early stuff, even the novellas he wrote under a fake name, and I'd spent hours as a kid trying to light fires with my mind, looking at cars and dogs trying to figure out which ones might be secretly evil. I'd tried for years to get Hayden to read them, but there was the whole dyslexia thing, which I should have been more sensitive about. Just another thing to regret.

The comics and graphic novels were in the back of the store, so I walked quickly through the aisles, past the sci-fi and gaming sections, to avoid the manager. There weren't many people around, which hopefully meant I could read in peace. I thought I caught a glimpse of that short-haired girl who hung out with Eric, Jess, but when I turned around she was gone. Must have been imagining it—it was so rare to see girls here.

The fourth volume had just come out, and I gratefully settled into reading about Skinner Sweet, the first of the American vampire bloodline. The series was awesome because it combined all the goriness of the vampire legend with stories about the Wild West and other eras in American history. I'd never been much of a history buff, but it was way more fun learning about it when you thought about vampires being involved.

I was so engrossed in the story that I almost flung the book across the room when I felt someone tap me on the shoulder. Crap. The manager was going to kick me out. I got ready to plead with him to just let me finish this issue, and turned around.

There was no one there.

But then I heard Astrid laugh. "I can't believe that worked on you again!" She was on my other side.

"What a pleasant surprise," I said. And it was. I couldn't help but be happy to see her, no matter what other things I was worried about.

"Well, I was early, and I figured you might be here." She leaned over my shoulder to see what I was reading. "I don't want to interrupt you reading your weird vampire comic or anything, though."

"Not a problem," I said, and put it down so I could look at her. Today's outfit was a kind of ripped-up white shirt with a long, black, lacy skirt and high laced-up Doc Martens. There were black and white streaks in her hair to match, and her lips looked like a checkerboard: half black, half white on top, and reversed on the bottom. It looked like a lot of work, so I figured I probably shouldn't kiss her, since I'd mess it up.

But then she frowned a little, and I remembered the look on her face when she asked me why I hadn't made a move on her. Lipstick was fixable, right? I pulled her toward me and then leaned in. I was so glad I did, too, because when I pulled back she was smiling, and her lipstick was hilarious, all smudgy and swirly and gray. And she was laughing at me, too, since my mouth probably looked just like hers.

"Looks like you need a Kleenex," she said.

"More like a Wet-Nap."

But we both couldn't stop smiling.

"You two shopping, or just blocking the aisle?" I heard the manager say.

"Let's just get out of here," Astrid said. She grabbed my hand and dragged me out of the ITC, toward the Sweet Spot, a candy store just off the food court. It sold just about every kind of sugary thing you could imagine—there was a whole aisle of weird-colored M&M's, a row consisting solely of gummy candies, and a section devoted to chocolates from all over the world. Astrid made a beeline for the penny candy.

"This stuff is my favorite," she said. "When I was little, my dad used to drive us to the fanciest part of town for Halloween, because they had the best stuff. This one house always gave out whole bags of old-school candy—saltwater taffy, candy necklaces, caramel bull's-eyes. I think they owned a restaurant or something."

"That was smart. We always stayed local. All Milky Ways and Almond Joys, and I hate coconut. Mom used to steal all my Reese's peanut butter cups—she called it rent."

We both bought our bags of candy and then sat down in the food court. "So there's something I have to ask you," I said.

"Sounds serious," she said, but I could tell she didn't really think so.

"Athena," I said. "The password. How did you know about that?"

The screen fell again, but I was determined to get past it.

"I really need to know," I said. "I'm going a little crazy here. I still feel like what happened to Hayden is my fault, but then there's all this other stuff with Jason and Trevor, and I just don't know what to do."

"You never finished telling me why you think it's your fault," she said.

"You're avoiding the question."

"So are you."

We stared at each other, almost as if daring the other one to talk first.

"Fine," I said. "I'll tell you the rest, if you promise to tell me about Athena."

"Fine," she said, and stuck a peppermint stick in her mouth without looking at me.

So Hayden and I had finally gone to a party, at his urging, no less, and here we were, lying on the ground, being laughed at. It was like living in a nightmare. I grabbed Hayden's arm and tried to pull him upright. "We've got to get out of here."

For some reason he resisted me, pulling his arm back but not getting up himself.

"Come on!" I said, and reached for him again.

This time he snatched his arm back. "Don't touch me," he said, but he did get up.

"What is going on with you? Are you okay?" I asked, trying to ignore the laughter around me, trying to pretend people weren't still looking at us.

"No, I'm not okay," he said. There was a ring of open space around us, but the path to the front door was packed with people. Hayden shoved his way through as the laughter died down; I followed him outside. The air had grown sharp and cold.

"Tell me what's going on," I said. "I don't understand. What just happened?"

"Nothing." He started walking quickly, almost as if he wanted to get away from me, though we were both going back to his house.

I walked faster, to catch up with him. I had the advantage because my legs were so much longer; he'd never be able to ditch me. "You can't say that was nothing. Why did we come here?"

"Why did we come here?" he repeated. "Why? For a public shaming, that's why."

I was starting to get angry. It was one thing for him not to tell me why before, but I'd been just as embarrassed as he was. He owed me. I'd just gone to a party I hadn't wanted to go to, gotten mocked by people I hated, realized nothing was ever going to change. And maybe that wasn't Hayden's fault, but right now it felt like it was. "You know, all you want to do most of the time is sit around and play Mage Warfare, and these days not even with me, and then you drag me to this party and we're not even there for an hour before we're both like five seconds away from getting our asses kicked by your stupid brother and his stupid friends. Who weren't even supposed to be there. And you still don't think it's worth telling me why the fuck we were even here in the first place?"

"You wouldn't understand," he said.

"Try me."

He shook his head. "I can't. Not now."

"I don't get it. You're my best friend. My only friend. I tell you everything, and you don't seem to trust me at all."

"It's not about trust!" he said, and I could tell he was getting angry too. "Maybe it's that once in a while I'd like something that's just mine. Not ours to share. Just something that's all about me. Why is that so hard to understand?"

It wasn't—I got it, really. In some ways that's what I wanted, too. "I just don't see why you can't have something that's yours but tell me about it anyway."

"I would have," he said. "But now it's gone."

"Would you stop it with the cryptic bullshit and just tell me already?" I yelled as we crossed the street.

He stopped in the middle of the road and turned to face

me. "No!" he screamed. "No, I'm not going to tell you. Wasn't it enough that I got thrown down the stairs and humiliated in front of everyone? Do I have to live through the rest of it again? I don't think so." He got out his wallet, pulled out a twenty, and threw it at me. "Here. You've got your phone. Call a cab. I want to be alone tonight."

The twenty fluttered to the ground in front of me. I didn't know what to do. I'd never seen him like this before, and truth be told, I didn't really want to go back to his house and have to deal with it. But I didn't want to have to pick up that twenty, either. I'd rather walk, no matter how far it was.

We stared at each other for a minute that felt like ten; the glare of headlights at a stop sign down the street finally snapped us out of it. We both started walking, in opposite directions.

"Fuck you, Hayden," I said, but he didn't turn around.

That was the last time I saw him. Alive, anyway.

I took a deep breath and waited for Astrid to say something. For a minute she sat there, sucking on that stupid peppermint stick, still not looking at me. Great. Now she understood. "See?" I said, eventually. "It really was my fault."

"It wasn't," she said.

"You can't say that."

"I can," she said, and then she finally looked at me. "I know why Hayden went to the party."

22
"LAST GOODBYE"
JEFF BUCKLEY

I STARED AT ASTRID LIKE AN IDIOT. "How could you know? You weren't there."

"I was supposed to be," she said.

I didn't know what to think. But the wheels in my head were spinning, spitting out possible scenarios. Astrid was Athena, and they were supposed to be together at the party. Athena was fake, and Ryan and his friends had set Hayden up just to embarrass him. But how would Astrid know that? Unless she'd been back with Ryan. God, I hoped that wasn't true. But it didn't seem right. Nothing I could think of seemed right.

"Let me tell you the whole thing," she said. She looked worried—scared, even—but she started talking anyway. "I told you I'd become friends with Hayden when I was going out with Ryan, but we stayed in touch even after the breakup. Just the occasional text here and there; he knew I was having a hard time with everything, and he was such a sweet kid. And I liked him so much. I didn't know why he always seemed so alone to me. Especially when he had a friend like you."

Something about the way she said it made me feel guilty, but I resolved to just listen and not try to defend myself.

"I decided he needed a girlfriend. And I told him that, but he was too shy to try himself."

I could have told her that; we'd talked about girls all the time, but neither of us had the guts to ever approach one.

"I wanted to fix him up, but I didn't think he'd go for it. So I figured I'd try another approach. I had the perfect person in mind: someone cute and small and shy, just like him. Someone creative, who could be talked into finding online gaming fun."

"Who?" I asked.

"Jess," Astrid said quietly, looking down.

I remembered the pixie-haired girl I'd seen at the party, and then at lunch, the one who'd never talked to me. I'd thought maybe she didn't like me for some reason; maybe she'd thought I was the one who hurt the bullies. But maybe it was just shyness. "Jess?"

Astrid nodded. "She's a sweetheart, just like Hayden, but she's even shyer than he is. I've been wanting the two of you to become friends, but the thought of it completely freaks her out, so I haven't pushed it. It's partly because I feel so awful about what happened. See, when you say it's your fault, I can say that I know it isn't. Because it's mine."

I started to shake my head.

"At least partially," she said. "I told her how into Mage Warfare Hayden was, that she should set up a user name and find him in the game. That way she wouldn't have to talk to him in person, not right away; I knew she was much more comfortable online, just like him. She was nervous at first, but I really talked Hayden up, and eventually she was into it. I even suggested the user name."

I felt my shoulders slump with relief. So that was the connection between Astrid and Athena. I had to admit, it made more sense than the thought of Hayden and Astrid together. And now I didn't have to feel weird about the idea of sharing a girlfriend with Hayden.

"It worked perfectly at first," she continued. "Hayden didn't tell me anything, of course; he wasn't about to confess to me when he hadn't even told you. But I kept up with Jess. She was so excited—it seemed like she was really coming out of her shell. They were super cute, always talking about music and making little mixes for each other. I felt like the world's best matchmaker. And I was even more excited when Jess told me they'd decided to meet in person. She'd been texting me while they were talking online, and I told her about the party. I figured Ryan and those guys wouldn't be there because of the football game, and I swore to her that it was the perfect place for them to meet. She was terrified he wouldn't be into her once he'd met her, though I knew there was no chance of it. But if that's what she needed to feel safe, then I'd make sure she had it. I'd be her wingman."

"But you weren't," I said.

She shook her head. "I wasn't. I was supposed to meet her there, but something happened, and I just couldn't. I apologized to her about a thousand times and promised her everything would be fine. Stephanie Caster's kind of a bitch, but her parties always draw such a big crowd that I figured Jess and Hayden could slip off together and no one would care. I knew it didn't really matter where they were; as soon as they met in person everything would be fine. She was nervous, but she said she'd be okay."

"What happened?" I asked. "Why didn't you go?"

"I can't talk about that," she said. "I'm sorry, but it's not my story to tell. Just trust me when I say I didn't have much choice. You know what it's like to have a best friend."

That meant it had to do with Eric. I wanted to believe her, but I just wasn't sure yet. "I don't remember seeing Jess at the party either, though."

"She got there before you guys did," Astrid said. "And it was just long enough for her to run into Ryan and his buddies." She said their names with even more bitterness in her voice than I usually had. She must really still hate him. "I don't know what they said to her, but whatever it was, it was enough to send her flying out of there. She texted me that she was breaking up with Hayden and she never wanted to hear his name again. I didn't get the message until hours later; I tried to ask her what happened but she wouldn't text me back."

"And Hayden never got to meet her."

"Which is just so sad to me," she said. "They could have been happy. If I'd gone to the party . . ."

"You know things wouldn't have been any different," I said. But I understood why she was sad; I felt the same way. Hayden had come so close to something real, and to have it taken away from him . . . that had to have been devastating.

"Not necessarily. I could have kept Jess away from those guys, or talked to her after, or kept them away from Hayden . . ."

"You can't know that. You can't know that anything would have been different."

"Well, neither can you," she said, and I supposed on some level she was right. "All we can say for sure is that Ryan and his friends are at least partly to blame."

I wanted so badly to ask whether she thought I was somehow taking revenge, but I didn't know how to say it without sounding crazy. And even as I got angrier and angrier at them, at whatever it was they'd said that pushed Hayden over the edge, I wanted desperately to know that I wasn't responsible. Maybe they deserved payback, but not this anonymous, physical harm. They needed to know they'd done something wrong. And everyone else needed to know it, too.

No, it couldn't have been me. It just couldn't have. But if not me, then who? Archmage_Ged? Really?

Astrid reached out and put her hand on mine. "Where are you, Sam? I lost you there for a minute, didn't I?"

"I'm just thinking," I said. "There's still so much that doesn't make sense to me, and there's still one thing I'm worried about. There's only one member of the bully trifecta who hasn't gotten what's coming to him: Ryan." I told her my theory, that if Jason and Trevor had been attacked, then Ryan was next.

She pulled at one of her hair extensions. "You can't be sure of that," she said. "It's not a given that the attacks are connected. It might be karma, but it could still be random, couldn't it?"

"It could, but that doesn't mean it is," I said. "I'm worried something will happen." I paused. "I mean, what if it really was me?"

"Not a chance," she said. "I know it wasn't. And so what if something happens to Ryan? He deserves whatever he gets."

"That's kind of harsh, isn't it?" It freaked me out a little that she could feel such hostility toward someone she used to like so much, but then again, I'd never been through a breakup before. I had no idea what it would be like, and I didn't want to have to think about it. I was glad she was so sure it wasn't me, though. I wanted to be that sure too.

"Do you really think so? Wouldn't you like to see all three of them get what they deserve? Wouldn't it be kind of satisfying, in a way?" She was leaning forward now, almost as if to say it was okay for me to say it, that she wouldn't judge me.

But I'd judge myself. I had to make sure things didn't go any further; I just didn't know how. "I don't think that would fix anything," I said.

"You never know," she said, and stood up. "I've got to head out now, but what are you doing this weekend?"

"I'm supposed to go to this mud racing thing with Rachel and her boyfriend, but if you want to hang out I can get out of it."

"No, that's perfect!" she said, finally smiling again. "That's what I was going to ask you about. Eric's racing. It'll be amazing."

"Eric?" I was still having trouble reconciling hipster Eric with farm-kid Eric, though I supposed the mudding thing made sense for someone who knew how to fix a tractor.

"He's shockingly good at it. And I think he's going to race Ryan. It'll be fun to see Eric kick his ass."

"Not sure 'fun' is the word I'd use, but I'll be there," I said.

And then we kissed, for a long time. I wished it were forever; I wished I could freeze that moment, standing in the middle of the mall, and not have to think about anything else ever again. I didn't want to think that Ryan was next, and that on Saturday, everyone would be watching. And I had no idea what was going to happen.

23 ▶

"HURT"

NINE INCH NAILS

SOMETHING ABOUT KNOWING ASTRID really and truly believed that I wasn't the one who'd attacked Jason and Trevor seemed to give me permission to finally get some much-needed rest. I managed to put everything out of my mind and just sleep, and it felt wonderful. I woke up the next morning feeling more awake and alert than I'd felt in weeks.

But the questions weren't gone. I wasn't sure what to do next until I remembered the thing that Astrid hadn't explained: why she hadn't gone to the party. It wasn't her story to tell, she'd said. Clearly, then, it was Eric's. I needed to talk to him.

The key was figuring out how to get Eric by himself—today was one of the days we all had lunch together. I scoured the cafeteria as soon as I got there, not bothering with food, and managed to catch Eric in line before he'd even sat down. "Can we talk for a minute?" I asked. "Alone?"

Eric smiled. "Looking for some dish on Astrid? I'm all yours."

Not even close, but I saw no need to say that right away. I steered him to a table in the opposite corner, where the rest of their crew wouldn't see us. Eric put his tray down but moved it aside a little; I almost felt bad that he seemed so excited to help me make things work with Astrid when there was a good chance I was going to ruin everything by opening my mouth. But I had to know.

I wasn't sure where to start, though. "Things have been really . . . complicated . . . for me since Hayden died," I finally said. "There's a lot going on, and I have a lot of questions. I thought maybe you could help me."

"I can try," he said. "Although I didn't really know Hayden. I knew Astrid wanted him to come hang out with us eventually, but she said he was shy, wasn't ready yet."

"My questions aren't really about Hayden. Not directly, anyway."

Eric gave me a quizzical look.

"I know this is going to sound kind of random, but I was talking to Astrid, and she was telling me about the night Hayden died. How she was supposed to go to that party, but she didn't. And I got the sense that maybe . . . maybe she didn't go because of you."

Eric's face fell. "I see," he said.

"I get that we don't know each other that well, and it

sounds like this is probably pretty personal," I said. "But is there any chance you'd be willing to tell me what happened?"

He looked down at the table for a minute, then looked back up at me. I could tell he'd made some sort of decision. "I'll tell you whatever you want to know, but not here. Can you come by my house this afternoon? After school?"

"Sure," I said. Whatever the story was, it sounded like it was going to be a big deal. I could barely wait.

The minute the final bell rang I headed over to Eric's house. I remembered he had a car, so I figured if I walked I could be sure he'd beat me there. The ground was damp from all that rain the other night, which I supposed was a good sign for the whole mudding thing, but I was wearing an old pair of Chuck Taylors and they squeaked as I walked, Hayden's playlist, as always, on my iPod.

He'd included two versions of the song "Hurt"—one was the original Nine Inch Nails version, which he loved. He had a thing for goth stuff; he went through a horrible Marilyn Manson phase that I wasn't sure our friendship would survive. He was convinced in particular of Trent Reznor's genius. I, on the other hand, didn't think I was even capable of liking a Nine Inch Nails song until I heard Johnny Cash's cover of "Hurt," the second version Hayden had included. Johnny Cash had covered a whole bunch of songs you wouldn't expect—Depeche Mode, Tom Petty, that sort of thing. I thought it was brilliant; Hayden thought it was a stunt he'd been talked into when he was getting ready to die. I'd softened my position on Trent Reznor eventually; I thought it was cool that he'd let Nine Inch Nails go for a while so he could score movies. Hayden had never wavered on the Johnny Cash covers, though, and the fact that he'd included both songs seemed like a sign to me, that he didn't totally hate me. Although I knew I was in constant danger of reading too much into the playlist. I wished I could feel more sure about why Hayden had included what he did, what it all meant, what he thought I would eventually be able to understand.

I finally got to Eric's house; his mom must have been out with the kids because he was the one who answered the door when I knocked. "Come on up," he said, and I followed him to the attic.

"Want something to drink?" He walked over to a mini-fridge and pulled out two bottles of water. I nodded, and he handed me one. "Let's get comfortable," he said. "We might be a while."

The piles of cushions and blankets were still strewn all over the floor from our movie night. Eric claimed a beanbag chair and I tried to stack up some pillows so I wasn't splayed out too awkwardly. I remembered how comfortable I'd felt the other day, curled up with Astrid; it was pretty much the opposite of how I felt right now.

I wasn't sure how to get him to start, so I figured I'd just start babbling and he could interrupt me. "I don't know how much Astrid's told you about me . . ."

Eric smiled. "Enough, that's for sure. She's very into you, in case you can't already tell."

I blushed. "Believe me, it's mutual. But you know about Hayden too, right?"

"I do," he said.

I appreciated that he didn't try to say more, that he just acknowledged that I'd lost something. It didn't make things better, but nothing would.

"She told me she was trying to help him," I said. "She was supposed to meet Jess at that party, but she didn't go."

"And that's where I come in," he said.

I was relieved that he understood. I waited for him to say more, but he seemed to be thinking. Then he took a long drink from his water bottle, like he was gearing up for something.

"What the hell," he said finally. "All my other friends know. And if you're going to be hanging out with us you might as well know too. Come take a look." He got up from the beanbag chair as gracefully as anyone can get out of a beanbag chair and walked over to the corner where he'd been painting the other day. I followed him and stared at the portrait, at those features that had looked so familiar, and then I realized why. I looked at Eric.

He nodded.

"That's Jason," I said.

"We used to be a thing," he said.

Of course. The rumor about Jason, Astrid mentioning that Eric had been through a bad breakup. But how could I have known? Just because they were both gay didn't mean they'd been a couple. They were such an unlikely pair.

We went and sat back down, and Eric started talking. "We met in church—we went to the same Sunday school class for years. And I think we probably both reacted the same way when the minister would rant and rave about the evils of homosexuality and all that. We were both closeted, though he was way more scared of people finding out than I was. I just figured it was no one's business but mine, and I wasn't ready to talk to my family yet. But his family was super religious, and he figured they'd completely freak out if they knew about him. Not to mention that even though they live on the east side, they have, like, no money, and he was counting on this church scholarship to go to college. If they found out he was gay, there was no chance he'd get it."

So that's what he'd meant the other day: *Most people around here would rather stay closeted than run the risk of losing a scholarship because your church found out you were gay.* I'd assumed he'd just been making an offhand comment, but he'd really been talking about Jason.

Eric paused to take another sip of water, and I realized on some level he wanted to tell the story to someone, start to finish, the way he'd probably not been able to before.

"That must have been really hard for both of you," I said.

"It was," he said, sounding grateful. "I know he can be a real asshole, but he wasn't like that when we were alone. He was different. It's hard to explain. But we were happy. At least I thought we were."

"But something happened," I said. "The night of Stephanie Caster's party." That must have been the night they broke up, but I didn't want to say it out loud.

"The very same," he said. "I still don't know all the details—Jason and I haven't so much as looked at each other since. But I can guess. I think his friends found out, and they freaked. Told him if he wanted to hang out with them, he had to end it, and no one could ever find out. So he did. Via an extremely unpleasant text message." He laughed, but it was a dark, ugly laugh.

"And that's why you called Astrid?"

"No, I knew she had that party to go to, and it sounded like it was really important for her to be there—I didn't know the details. But I guess Trevor and Ryan thought it wasn't enough that Jason break up with me; they had to make sure to keep me busy enough not to try and get him back."

I wasn't sure what he meant. "How?"

"They outed me to my parents. That was when I snapped. I wanted to call Astrid, but I was hysterical. I could barely talk I was crying so hard."

Something about that made me almost jealous; I

wondered if it was because I hadn't yet been able to cry for Hayden.

"I picked the girls up but I still couldn't talk," he said. "I think Astrid thought something had happened to me, like physically. When we got to the party she refused to get out of the car; she told Jess that it would be okay, that she'd be there soon, but she needed some time with me. I didn't ask her to stay, but in a lot of ways I'm really grateful she did, even though I know it screwed everything up. I still feel guilty about that."

You and me both, I thought, but I didn't say it. I didn't know what to say, really. I thought about when I'd said something about Eric's family accepting him, how Astrid had said, "They do now," and Eric had basically shut her down. I'd stepped in it without realizing, and I didn't want to do it again. "I'm sorry," I said.

"Thanks. It's okay now—it's not like I wasn't going to tell them; I just wanted to do it on my own time, in my own way. They're not homophobes or anything; they just haven't been around gay people all that much, and it's taking them some time to get used to the idea that their firstborn isn't what they thought he was. But in some ways it's made my life easier—now I don't have to worry all the time about people finding out, and I can dress and act how I want."

Like Astrid, I thought. "I'm guessing you're not thanking those guys for the opportunity, though."

"Hardly," he said. "Like I told you the other day, I'm fine with them getting what they deserve. To a point." It was an odd thing to say, and I wasn't sure how to take it. "But that's partly why I'm so excited about the race tomorrow. I'm going to destroy Ryan, even with him driving Trevor's fancy new truck. He has no idea what he's getting into."

That's exactly what I was worried about. I wasn't sure how to ask what I really wanted to know. I mean, I'd been looking for someone else who had a vendetta against the trifecta, and now I'd found him. Did that mean I had the answer to my question? Did that mean I finally knew who was behind the attacks?

Except the way he talked about what happened—he sounded kind of like me. And if we both thought things had gone a little too far, did it make sense for either of us to be responsible? "You're going to destroy him at the race," I said, hoping he would understand.

"Yes, at the race," he said, and I thought maybe he did. "I can beat him, because he sucks, and he thinks Trevor's truck is like, magical or something, but it isn't, and this is the one place I can completely humiliate him on his own terms, and I'm going to do it. And that's what I need to focus on right now."

He sounded like me again. We both wanted Ryan to get what he deserved, but in public. Where everyone would know exactly what happened. Still, I had to be sure.

“Fair and square?” I said.

“Fair and square,” he said. “I mean it. This kind of thing can be really dangerous if you screw around.” I remembered that stupid TV show that got canceled when a bunch of dudes got trapped in their truck.

“I wasn’t sure how worried you were about things being dangerous,” I said.

He gave me a look, and now I was sure he knew what I was talking about. “I worry,” he said quietly. “More than you think.”

“I’m glad,” I said. “Good luck.” I still wasn’t as sure as I wanted to be—if it wasn’t me and it wasn’t Eric, I was at a loss to think of who was left, but I wanted to believe there could be someone else. And I really wanted to believe that the only bad thing that was going to happen to Ryan was that he was going to lose the race. I hoped it was true.

And I was looking forward to being there to see it.

24

"FOR EMMA"

BON IVER

RACHEL TOOK ONE LOOK AT ME as I came downstairs Saturday afternoon and sent me back upstairs to change. "Which part of 'mudding' did you not understand? You're going to be covered. Find something crappier."

I wasn't exactly dressed fancy, but when I saw Rachel and Jimmy I understood. They were both wearing all black, with raincoats and big clunky boots—Rachel's were rubber, Jimmy's were combat, duh—and while I wasn't familiar enough with Jimmy's wardrobe to tell, I knew Rachel's clothes were really old; I recognized her leggings as ones she usually reserved for use as pajamas. I put on an old sweatshirt, my oldest jeans, and winter boots and got the nod from Rachel.

"What exactly is happening here?" Mom asked. "You all look ridiculous."

I didn't point out that, as far as I was concerned, Rachel and Jimmy tended to look kind of ridiculous all the time. Not to mention that Mom was wearing her work outfit; her scrubs today were covered with little ducks.

She must have seen me looking at her. "Don't say it," she warned, and then turned to Jimmy. "Drive safe," she said. "You've got my whole life in your car."

Jimmy gestured as if tipping his chauffeur hat. "I'm on it, Mrs. Goldsmith."

We still had a few days to go before Halloween, but the air was chilly, and Rachel's hair tangled in the wind as we walked outside to Jimmy's car. I wished I'd brought a coat, but I had a long-sleeved T-shirt on under my sweatshirt, and I hoped it would be enough. "You're sure this is a good idea?" I asked as I got into the backseat, surprisingly clean given how much trash was in the front.

"Don't ask me," Jimmy said. "This was all your sister's idea."

"You need to get out more," Rachel said. "And won't your girlfriend be there?"

"We haven't exactly formalized our relationship," I said, but I blushed anyway. So annoying.

We passed the rest of the drive quietly, listening to Jimmy's radio blaring out some whiny-voiced old singer wailing about Tom Sawyer over the insistent screeching of several guitars. I tried to block it out of my head by thinking about Hayden's playlist; my favorite song on it was by Bon Iver, a band that was really just one guy, but he had this amazing high voice—not anxious and jangly like the guy singing now, but soft and throaty, almost feminine. Hayden had been pretty aggressively not into it when I'd made him listen, but he'd softened his stance over time, and I wasn't surprised to hear a song about lost love on the mix, not after everything I'd learned.

It took about twenty minutes to get to wherever it was we were going. I wasn't sure whether to think of it as a party or a drag race or what, but regardless, we ended up deep in a field that I was guessing had recently been stripped of soybeans—it was too flat for corn. The rain from the other day had left it nice and muddy, more so than some of the other fields we'd passed.

The real benefit of this area, though, was that the field bordered a large expanse of trees, which blocked the field from the road and provided some shelter in case it started to rain again. I could see that some people had started a bonfire in an expanse between two patches of trees, and there were a couple of kegs set up nearby. There were already at least thirty or forty kids milling around the area where the kegs were set up; I was relieved to see that Rachel was right, that there were people from all different social groups here, and everyone seemed to be getting along fine.

Next to the kegs was a kind of makeshift parking lot with a bunch of cars in it, and then, of course, there were the trucks. At least ten of them, lined up on the side of the field, where a long piece of white tape marked what apparently was going to function as a starting line.

"There's a finishing line way out that way," Rachel said, pointing. "Check out the middle, though—that's where the action's going to be."

I followed her finger to a spot I had to strain to see at first but that I could tell was the wettest part of the field—the ground had sunk a bit, and the fading sun glistened on pools of oily water, making little rainbows like I used to love seeing in parking-lot puddles as a kid.

I looked back over the row of trucks. It was easy to pick out Trevor's, the red monstrosity covered with obnoxious bumper stickers. IF AT FIRST YOU DON'T SUCCEED, MAYBE YOU'RE A LOSER, and LOST YOUR CAT? TRY LOOKING UNDER MY TIRES. Classy.

A few trucks down was a more modest-looking pickup, one that I could picture actually hauling stuff on a farm, a faded blue Ford with patches of rust. Must have been Eric's.

"Looks like everyone's over by the kegs," Jimmy said.

"Might as well drink up," Rachel said. "It's cold, and things won't get going for another hour or so."

I remembered the party: the beers had helped, until I'd gotten too drunk. The trick for me seemed to be to nurse beer and stay away from the whiskey. I followed them past the trucks, looking for Astrid and her friends, but it took me a minute to find them; I saw Damian's beard, then Jess standing next to him. Astrid and Eric were standing a few feet away; Astrid's long platinum-blond hair was free of streaks and bundled into some kind of knot on the top of her head. She was whispering something to Eric, who looked angry, and grabbed her arm. She pulled away from him and stormed off, ducking behind the back of the row of trucks until it was hard to see her. "Actually, I'll meet you guys over there, okay?" I said.

I walked back to the row of trucks, where Astrid was kneeling behind Trevor's, pulling things I couldn't quite see out of that bronze backpack of hers and piling them on the ground. "Hey," I said.

She looked up, startled. "Sam! I didn't expect to see you here yet." She stood up and put her hands on her hips, almost as if to block my view of her backpack. But it was too late.

"Apparently," I said, and gestured to the pile. "What are the potatoes for, Astrid?"

She twitched as if I'd hit her. I saw several expressions flicker across her face. Trying to figure out what approach to take, I figured. "I'm so glad it's you!" she finally said. "Going old school for this one—potatoes in the exhaust pipe. If you stuff a few in there, they should shoot out when Ryan revs the engine. It'll make a huge boom and scare the crap out of him. Then Eric can run him down for real. If he cooperates. It'll be amazing."

It took me a minute to process everything she was saying.

For this one? Run him down for real?

I'd done some research before I talked to Eric, just to see what kinds of pranks someone could pull in a situation like this; I'd read a million articles on the potato thing. Which meant I knew that the potato thing itself wasn't going to work; either the potatoes would fall out or the truck wouldn't start. There was like a one-in-a-million chance that the potatoes would actually shoot out like she thought, but even if they did, they could really hurt someone.

Was that what she wanted?

My mind was racing; I could feel that my mouth had dropped open, and I probably looked like an idiot, but I couldn't help myself. Because finally I was putting it together.

"For this one," she'd said.

Time for act three.

I wasn't sure whether I wanted to yell or run away. My ears were ringing even though neither one of us had said anything for at least a minute. No, not you, I thought. I'd wanted it to be someone else, but not like this. Finally some words came out, in almost a whisper. "It was you? All along?"

"At your service," she said, with a little bow. She was trying to sound casual, but I could see her starting to shake. I couldn't even imagine what she was seeing in my face now.

"I don't— I can't—" I didn't know what to say. I didn't even know where to start.

"God, Sam, I thought of all people you'd understand,"

Astrid said. Her lip curled up and I couldn't tell if she was sneering or trying to keep from crying.

"You let me think it was me!"

"Come on, you couldn't really have thought that." But there was a catch in her voice; she was trying to sound tough, but it wasn't working.

"You have no idea what I was thinking," I said, and I knew it was true. All this time I'd thought we'd understood each other, but I'd been wrong all along.

"Besides, it was better if you didn't know," she said. "You couldn't get in trouble if you didn't know the details. And I really liked hanging out with you, getting to know you—I thought you'd get it, but I wanted to be sure. I dropped enough hints; I thought you'd figured it out."

I thought back on our conversations about karma. Had it just been her code for telling me all along? Her way of telling me not to worry, that I hadn't done it? That she had me covered? It couldn't be.

"Was it just you? Was it Eric, too?"

"Not exactly," she said. She sounded calm; apparently if she'd had the urge to cry, it had passed. "He drove the night I got Trevor. But he was kind of pissed at how it all went down. I don't think he realized just how mad I was. It's a good thing I didn't need his help—it's not as hard as you think to knock someone out when they don't see you coming."

The baseball bat probably contributed to that, I thought. "What about Jason?" I asked. "Eric said he hadn't seen him since they broke up. Was he lying?"

She shook her head. "Damian helped out with that one. We were so angry at what Jason and those guys did to Eric that we had to do something."

"So none of this is about Hayden at all?" It was bad enough that Astrid was behind all of this, but somehow the idea that it was unconnected to Hayden made it worse.

"Of course it's about Hayden," she said. "That means Ryan's the most important, for his sake and mine. But this part won't work without Eric. I've been trying to make him see that, but he's obsessed with taking Ryan down on his own."

I took a step back, almost involuntarily. I felt the need to be farther away from her.

"Oh, come on, Sam," she pleaded. "Don't be like that. You know they're monsters. They ruined Eric's life, and Hayden's, and Jess's, and mine. And yours. They were destroying everything they touched and no one was doing a damn thing about it. I'm so sick of them being able to get away with it. Someone had to do something. You have to understand that." She reached out toward me, as if to take my hand.

But I pulled back farther. "You hurt people," I said. "Badly." My voice was getting louder.

"They deserved to be hurt. A lot worse than anything I did. Jason mostly just got humiliated, and Trevor's going to be fine."

"What about what you were planning with Ryan? What did you think would happen, if it worked?" Now I was yelling. People were starting to look.

She shrugged.

"Did you even care?" My voice cracked. I couldn't remember ever being this angry. Not at someone I could confront.

I'd been so worried that I was responsible, and then that Eric was, that it hadn't even occurred to me to consider the possibility of Astrid being involved. To think about how I might feel. But now I knew.

It was awful.

It was so awful that it overshadowed my relief at the knowledge, finally, that it hadn't been me.

Astrid must have seen something in my face. "I did it for Hayden," she said softly.

As if that made it better. But it wasn't even true, not really. "You did it for yourself," I said, just as quietly.

She looked at me, as if trying to think of the words that would fix things. But there weren't any. I felt like everything I knew about her had turned out to be a lie. I'd thought we were the same, that we'd been lucky to find each other, especially now, but maybe it wasn't good luck. Maybe this was just another horrible way of reminding me that I really had lost the only true friend I'd ever had.

There wasn't really anything I wanted to say to her, except one thing. "Please don't do this," I said. "Let Eric handle this his own way."

She nodded, then knelt back down and started picking up the potatoes and putting them back in her bag. "I thought you'd understand," she said, not looking at me now.

In some ways I did, but not in the ways that mattered. She wasn't who I thought she was, who I'd wanted her to be. And now I had to face being alone again.

I walked away.

I hadn't asked Astrid a lot of the questions I'd meant to; I wanted to know how much Eric knew, if her other friends did too, why she'd decided it was her job to take the bullies down in the first place. But did it matter? I'd lost her—or she'd lost me, really—and with that, I'd lost the prospect of a new group of friends. Maybe the problem was the whole idea of groups; as soon as more than two people got involved in anything, so many things could go wrong. There was the bully trifecta, three idiots all but sharing one brain; Astrid's old cheerleader friends, who'd dumped her when Ryan did; her new friends, helping her plot revenge against the bullies without even seeming to realize that they were condoning violence themselves. I was almost inclined to think that what they were doing was worse—there was no question what the bullies were, because they did most of their harm in the open, but Astrid's crew did everything in stealth, leaving someone like me to take the blame.

Who needed a group? What was so bad about having one best friend, anyway?

I missed Hayden as much as I had since he died. I missed him so much I finally didn't even feel bad thinking about it; I just sank into it, let it roll over me in waves. It was the closest I'd come to crying, and if I hadn't been like two feet away from a field full of people I mostly didn't know or couldn't stand, I might have just said fuck it and started bawling.

I didn't, though. Not that I cared so much about what any of those people thought of me most of the time, but I had some pride. And there was no way, absolutely no fucking way, I was going to stand around crying in a cornfield—soybean field, whatever—and let Astrid and her friends think she'd reduced me to tears. But I couldn't seem to manage standing up anymore; I let myself fall to my knees and stared at the ground, trying to pretend everyone else was gone. I heard the song I'd been thinking about in the car playing over and over in my mind, with its references to loving people who lied to you. That wasn't going to be me. I was done with lies, with secrets and hidden things. I would get over Astrid, in a way I might never get over losing Hayden. I was fine with being alone.

And then I felt the tap on my shoulder.

25

"COSMIC LOVE"

FLORENCE AND THE MACHINE

I COULDN'T IMAGINE ASTRID would have dared come back. But I braced myself when I looked up, just in case. No Astrid, though. Just a small, scared-looking girl with short spiky hair.

Jess.

"Can I talk to you?" she asked. Her voice was high pitched and as quiet as I'd have expected from someone as shy and withdrawn as she seemed to be.

I stood up. I must have been a foot taller than her. "Sure," I said, trying to sound like someone who had his composure, which I was not. "Do you mind if we go over by the bonfire, though? I'm freezing." It was true; the air had gotten even colder as the sky darkened, and my sweatshirt wasn't nearly warm enough. But really, I didn't want to be able to see Astrid.

She looked up at me and gave a little nod. We walked closer to the fire, where it was warmer, and found a dry patch on the ground to sit.

"Are you okay?" Jess asked.

She must have seen everything, so she had to know I wasn't. But I didn't want to think about that; I wanted to know why she'd asked to talk to me. Now that we were right next to each other I had a chance to see her more clearly, to imagine how Hayden would have seen her. She wasn't a particularly pretty girl; everything about her was tiny, almost too much so. Her eyes were small and set close together; her mouth so little that her lips were just two thin lines. Her hair was clipped short and I could see her miniscule ears, their lobes just barely large enough to contain her stud earrings. "I'll be okay," I said, and I wanted it to be true.

She looked back at me, and I became aware that I was staring. But then she gave me a shy smile, and I got it. I could see why Astrid had imagined them together, could see how she and Hayden fit, how her size would make him feel strong. And they'd fallen for each other without ever having met in person; I had no idea whether Jess had asked Astrid to point Hayden out, but if she had, clearly she'd found him appealing in some way. I'd always thought people who started relationships online were nuts, but now I wondered if they knew something I didn't. There was something so pure about it, how Hayden and Jess had based everything they felt on who they were, on who they knew the other person to be, and maybe they'd been right.

"Astrid talks about you all the time," Jess finally said,

softly. "And he did too. I'm glad we have a chance to talk. I thought maybe if I explained things to you, you'd understand a little better."

I understood why she didn't want to say Hayden's name out loud. She was dead wrong if she thought she was going to change my mind about what I'd just learned, though. But I didn't want to stop her from telling her story. "I wasn't sure you were real at first," I admitted. "When Astrid told me about Athena, I thought maybe it was her."

Jess laughed. "Hard to imagine," she said. "It took Astrid a long time to get over Ryan. I think maybe it didn't happen until Hayden told her about you." She swallowed a little after saying "Hayden," but it seemed to loosen her up.

"What do you mean?"

"She had a thing for you just based on what he'd told her, before you even met. I think she set me and Hayden up with the idea that someday it would be the four of us, together."

I felt my throat close as she said that. Why couldn't Astrid have found me sooner? Trusted me sooner? Maybe I could have stopped her from doing what she did. I don't know that I could have stopped her from wanting to, though, and right now that was the real problem. But I wasn't here to talk about Astrid. "Can you tell me what happened? At the party?"

"I figured that's what you wanted to know," Jess said. "Astrid told me you blame yourself for what happened. And I know she thinks she's responsible, too. But it wasn't either of your faults. It was mine."

"I find that hard to believe," I said.

"But I know what really happened. You only know what you saw at the party."

"Please," I said. "Tell me whatever you can."

She spoke slowly and softly, and I had to lean in to hear her.

"I had this idea that when Hayden actually saw me he'd change his mind and take off, and I couldn't bear the thought of it. I knew I had to meet him in public, so I could hide if something went wrong. Astrid said the party would be perfect. Hayden and I weren't sure; we weren't exactly party people. But Astrid assured me it would work—that girl's house was huge, and there were all these rooms where we could go off and talk, and it would be less awkward than just the two of us alone somewhere. If we met in person and it didn't feel the same, she would leave with me. Astrid and me spent the whole day together getting ready, and the plan was that Eric would pick us up and take us over there a little early, so we could get settled in. I'm not so great with crowds."

"Me neither," I said. I could hear the fire crackling.

"When Eric came to pick us up, he was a mess. Red eyes, mismatched clothes. He couldn't talk—he just drove us to the party and then indicated that we should get out; it was clear he wasn't coming. He held up his phone, like we should call him to pick us up. But Astrid wouldn't get out of the car."

"Yeah, he told me what happened," I said.

"I bet he didn't tell you how freaked out we were, though. You have to understand, Eric usually has it together. I'd never seen him like this, and I don't think Astrid had, either. She kept asking him if he needed anything, if he wanted to talk, and he kept shaking his head, but it was pretty clear that he was about to start crying again. She asked me if I'd be okay for a little while and I told her of course I would, that she should go talk to him. He needed her more. I'd manage at the party by myself until she could come back. She didn't want to go, but it was obvious that she had to."

"That's what she told me, but she made it sound like she ditched you."

"See, that's why she thinks it's her fault, and that's why she's wrong."

"Tell me the rest," I said, and shifted a little to get closer to the fire. I was still cold, though I wasn't sure how much of that was from the chill outside and how much was from how anxious I was to hear what had really happened.

"Eric dropped me off, and I thought I'd just go in and find a quiet place to hide until Hayden got there. Astrid had pointed him out to me at school, so I knew who he was even if he didn't know me. I was so excited to finally meet him, to introduce myself properly. And scared, too, but kind of in a good way."

"I get it," I said, and I did. "But I'm kind of confused about one thing. Why didn't you just meet him at school? I know you wanted to be somewhere public, and school's pretty public."

She looked down. "It's embarrassing," she said, and tugged on her earlobe. It reminded me of Astrid, pulling on her hair extensions. "It's just—I've never been on a date before, let alone kissed someone. And I know I'm weird-looking and quiet—"

You're not, I wanted to say, but she was, and we both knew it.

"—and I was scared. I was afraid Astrid had been wrong, that he wouldn't like me, and I'd gotten so attached to who we were online, I didn't want to mess it up. I knew it couldn't go on like that forever, but if something bad was going to happen, if he took one look at me and decided it wasn't going to work, I didn't want to have to get through the rest of school. I wanted to be able to just go home."

There were other, better ways, I thought, but then again, what did I know? "So why didn't you stay until we got there?"

"Because Ryan and his buddies got there first."

Of course.

"I don't know what his problem is, but he really has it in for Hayden," she said. "He'd found the chat logs—Hayden must have left the game open one day, and Ryan had gone in and read them."

"Maybe he saw Hayden looking happy for once," I said bitterly.

"Could be," she said, her tone matching mine. "Anyway, he must have seen me looking around, or even just looking totally out of place at that party, both of which were true—he came right up to me. 'You're Jess, aren't you?' he asked. I told him I was. He looked me up and down and started laughing. 'I'm Hayden's brother,' he said. 'He asked me to give you a message.'

"I got kind of excited. I didn't know much about Ryan, really; I knew he and Astrid had gone out but she didn't like to talk about it. And I knew he and Hayden didn't get along, but Hayden didn't say much about it either, and I thought maybe things had changed. Maybe Hayden being happier was helping him deal with his family." Her little mouth twisted. "Pretty presumptuous of me, right? To think I could make a difference to someone I hadn't even met?"

"But you did," I said.

Jess picked at a patch of dried grass from underneath her leg. "Well, I figured out pretty quickly that I didn't understand things at all," she said, with some bitterness. "Ryan's message for me was that Hayden had looked for me at school, now that he knew my real name. And he was horrified to think that I was who he'd been talking to. He wasn't coming."

"That wasn't true!" I yelled. "We were on our way!" I felt like I was watching one of those horror movies, where the viewer knows the killer is coming but the victim doesn't. I knew what was happening, but I was powerless to stop it. I wished there were some kind of rewind button I could press.

"Sure, I know that now," she said. "But you have to understand—it was exactly what I was afraid of. I'm sure Ryan had figured that out from the chat logs. He knew just how to hurt me, and he knew it would hurt Hayden, too. Who would be that cruel?"

"Someone who would out someone so he could keep pretending his friend wasn't gay," I said, and shook my head.

"I didn't want to believe it," Jess said. "But Ryan was laughing, and his friends backed him up, even as they saw me starting to cry. I had to get out of there, so I left. And then I sent Hayden a text."

Oh no. "What did it say?"

She looked down, and even in the dark I could see a tear drop from her eye onto the ground. She reached into her pocket and pulled out her phone. Then she showed me.

I CAN'T BELIEVE YOU WOULD DO THIS TO ME. YOU ARE THE MEANEST PERSON I HAVE EVER KNOWN. I'M GLAD WE NEVER MET IN PERSON. DON'T EVER CONTACT ME AGAIN.

I could see, below it, the string of responses from Hayden. Text after text, question after question, assurance after assurance that he had no idea what she was talking about. All unanswered.

"I didn't see them. I shut off my phone," she said, after she could tell I'd finished reading. "I was angry, and I lashed out, and I didn't want to hear what he had to say. I called a cab and went home alone. And it wasn't until the next day that I finally talked to Astrid, and I realized that they were lying. But by then it was too late."

She looked up at me. "You see it now? It's all my fault."

I felt such a mix of emotions. I felt terrible for Jess; I could see how sad she was, and I understood why she felt responsible, even though I could totally understand why she'd reacted as she did. But I also wished she'd done something, anything else, something that hadn't left Hayden thinking that it hadn't been real, because I was pretty sure that was what had broken him.

"Just look," Ryan had said. I realized he'd probably been talking about the text message.

And with that, the last hope Hayden had of his life being different, better, had disappeared. Really, it was Ryan's fault, more than anyone else's, even if Hayden hadn't known that. I was so angry I could feel the blood pumping through my veins. I wanted to kill him for taking my best friend away from me. And then I realized that this must have been exactly how Astrid felt.

But I didn't want to be like her. Hurting him wouldn't do me any good. Even just blaming him didn't make me feel any better. Who was I to say who was any more responsible than anyone else? I took a minute and waited for my pulse to slow.

Jess was still sitting there, looking at me, waiting for me to speak. Her eyes were starting to fill with tears, and I knew I had to say something, even if there wasn't much I could say that would help. After all, nothing anyone said to me had worked. "You know, if you're convinced it was your fault, and Astrid's convinced it's hers, and I'm convinced it's mine, maybe we all need to accept that none of us are going to be a hundred percent right. I don't think I'll ever stop blaming myself for my part, but in some ways it's easier to blame myself than anyone else, and maybe someday that will make it possible for me to let myself off the hook a little bit. Because if none of us is a hundred percent responsible, then it's probably just as likely that none of us could have stopped this from happening, even if we'd known what it was we should have been trying to do. And we probably need to accept that, just like we need to accept that he's not coming back."

I wasn't sure I'd made any sense, but Jess was nodding. And I realized, even as I was saying it, that it was true, though I also knew it wasn't going to make either of us feel better. Not for a long time. But I felt a small sense of community in my guilt and grief, with Jess, even with Astrid, even though I still couldn't process what she'd done.

We stood up and looked at each other for a minute, neither of us knowing what else there was to say. Then, almost as if she hadn't known she was going to do it, Jess reached out to hug me. I hugged her back, feeling her tiny collarbone against my rib cage. We stayed that way for so long it almost got awkward, but it didn't, and I felt this moment of relief that she really, truly understood everything.

We finally let each other go and walked out of the woods together, still not talking, but in a way that seemed comfortable and right. By the time we got back everyone was at the starting line; Jess walked over to Astrid and whispered something to her, and I could see Astrid leaning down to listen and nodding. They were a funny pair, Astrid so tall and Jess so little. Kind of like Hayden and me. Astrid looked over at me, and we stood there for a minute, our eyes locked. I looked away first.

Instead, I went and found Rachel and Jimmy. "Race is about to start, kiddo," Rachel said. "Let's go."

26

"THE MOTHER WE SHARE"

CHVRCHES

THE THREE OF US STAKED OUT a spot in the middle of the field, just outside the muddiest part of the path the trucks would follow. "This is why I made you change," Rachel said. "We're going to get slathered. It'll be amazing."

I wasn't seeing how, but it didn't matter. We weren't so far that I couldn't see the drivers getting in their trucks; it looked like Eric and Ryan were going first. I hadn't seen Ryan since the funeral, and it was kind of weird to see him alone, without Jason and Trevor—Trevor was probably still laid up, and Jason was laying low. Was I crazy, or was Ryan wearing one of Hayden's T-shirts? I tried to remember which ones had been in the box and realized I didn't remember seeing Hayden's old Smiths shirt. I could feel a vein in my temple starting to throb.

From the starting line I heard the trucks gearing up—the purr of Trevor's engine in that fancy new truck; the low rumbling of Eric's well-used family pickup. Then both of them revved their engines, and I could hear the power Ryan had at his disposal. How exactly did Eric think he could beat him?

I heard the shrill blare of a whistle, and then both trucks were off. They had a few hundred yards to get going, from what I could tell, and for that stretch Ryan was ahead, though not as much as I'd expected given how much newer and nicer Trevor's truck was.

It soon became clear, though, that the speed they'd built was only going to be so helpful once they reached the muddy part of the track. Both trucks hit the mud with their front tires spinning wildly, throwing mud on the throng of people who'd moved up to watch on both sides of the track. Rachel was right; within seconds just about everyone was covered. We all smelled like pig shit, which was completely gross at first, until my nose got used to it.

Once the trucks' back tires hit the mud, though, it seemed like the front tires became almost irrelevant as the trucks fought to keep their forward momentum. It was almost as if the mud was trying to actively slow them down and suck them under; the only way to get through was to maintain speed, but it was clear how hard that was to do.

This, I could tell, was where Eric had an edge—probably from driving in mud on the farm. "Trevor usually drives in these things," Rachel yelled to me, and I could see it—Eric obviously knew how it handled better than Ryan did. Ryan was trying to force the truck to move through the mud by going as fast as he could, but all he was doing was moving the mud around; the wheels spun and spun but the truck's progress was minimal. He wasn't stuck yet, but he wasn't moving very fast, either.

Eric's truck, in contrast, seemed to be gliding over the mud. It almost looked like he was doing an extended wheelie—the front wheels were almost off the ground, and the back wheels were the ones propelling the truck forward. It took me a minute to figure out why, partly because my eyes were half full of mud: Eric was subtly steering the truck left and right as he moved forward. Barely enough to be noticeable, but apparently enough to ensure the wheels had traction and to keep them from spinning out.

Eric's truck passed Ryan's just seconds before it became clear that Ryan had actually gotten Trevor's truck stuck in the mud. By the time Eric crossed the finish line Ryan hadn't managed to pull himself out, and finally he just killed the engine and got out. Eric and his crew celebrated at the finish line, whooping and singing and being silly in complete unabashed triumph. I watched them for a while and debated going over, but I didn't want to interrupt their party, and I didn't want to join it, either. Astrid was singing just as loudly as the rest of them; I looked as closely as I could for some sign that she was suffering, like I was, but I couldn't see any indication of it now.

A group of jocks had gathered around Trevor's truck, helping Ryan get it out of the mud. By the time they pushed it over the finish line, Eric and his friends had calmed down a little. Ryan leaned on the truck, covered in mud; Eric was the cleanest person around, other than spatter and handprints on his shirt from his friends hugging him or patting him on the back. I could see Eric and Ryan make eye contact as I walked toward the finish line—I was curious to see what would happen next.

For a while, neither of them said anything. It was like a game of chicken. Eric had won, and Ryan was obviously upset about it, but the pissing contest wasn't quite over. Whoever spoke first ran the risk of looking weak. From the look on Eric's face, I could tell he was fighting with himself. He wanted to say something, to force Ryan to acknowledge that he'd been beaten, that Eric had beaten him, but he was trying to be patient.

And then, to my surprise, Ryan stuck out his hand. "Good race," he said.

Eric cocked his head and stood there for a minute, clearly not sure what to do. He looked over at Astrid, who, I was surprised to see, was smiling. Why was it so important for everyone to get her approval? But that's what it must have been; Eric shook Ryan's hand and said, "You too."

From my perspective, it was a relief—it seemed as clear a

sign as any that the war was over, that I didn't have to worry about revenge plots anymore. I didn't have time to be relieved for long, though, because Ryan had left the finish line and was walking right toward me.

I'd been right; he was wearing Hayden's Smiths T-shirt. Funny how it fit him perfectly; I hadn't thought for a long time about how he and Hayden basically had the same build, though Ryan had converted his thickness to muscle. They even looked alike, though Ryan's features were sharper and handsomer than Hayden's. "Can we talk?" he asked. He sounded just like I had, when Jess came up to me—a little nervous, but determined.

I shrugged. I wasn't about to make things easy for him, whatever it was he wanted to say.

"We'll be here whenever you're ready," Rachel said.

We walked a few feet away; the next race was starting, so no one was paying any attention to us. "I've been thinking a lot about what you said at the funeral," Ryan said.

Seriously? Jason had practically dislocated my shoulder when he knocked me down. "You have a weird way of showing it," I said.

"My friends are very protective of me," he said. "They know I've been going through a lot."

"Sure you have," I said, feeling the anger rise up in me again. "Your life was pretty close to perfect, and now your geeky little brother won't get in the way."

He looked like I'd slapped him, and I wondered if I'd gone too far. "Look, I know you're Hayden's best friend, so you see things how he did. But did you ever think that maybe it was just one side of the story?"

"You're telling me there's two sides? You made his life hell, you stole his chance to have a girlfriend, and now he's dead. What's the other side?"

"You don't know what it was like for me," he said. "One of my earliest memories is of Dad puncturing my soccer ball with a steak knife so I would throw the football around with him. You think I wanted to play football, a guy my size? I get killed out there. I would have made a great goalie, but Dad said soccer was for wimps and he wasn't going to have a wimpy kid. At least not until Hayden, who got to just hide in his room playing video games all day. He didn't have to deal with any of our parents' crap."

Was he kidding? "Did you not hear how they talked to him?"

"Sure, talk," he said. "But at the end of the day, they left him alone. And Hayden had a learning disorder. They yelled at him about his grades, but they didn't hold him to the same standard they used for me. I had to get straight As or there was no allowance, no clothes for school, no new equipment for sports. I worked my ass off." He paused, wondering, I was sure, why he was bothering to tell me all this. I know I was. "It was just so unfair," he finally said, and his voice grew softer.

"I knew it wasn't his fault; I knew it was better for him to fight them and then hide out than to cave like I had. But God, I resented him so much for it. I get that it makes me a bad person. I get it."

I wasn't going to argue with him on that one. "Is that why you made Jess leave the party?"

"It's more complicated than that," he said. "I'd gone into his room to use his computer because mine crashed—you know I have an old shitty one because I keep getting Bs in math, and they won't upgrade it until I fix it—and I'd seen him talking to this girl online. And for some reason it just made me furious to think that he was going to meet this girl, when I'd lost the one girl I was really into."

"Astrid?"

He nodded. "I know you've been hanging out with her, and she probably told you what an asshole I am for dumping her, but you have no idea what it was like when her dad died. I guess I understand it better now, but she turned into a totally different person, and it was like every decision she made was a judgment on what she'd been like before. And on me. So I broke up with her, but really, she broke my heart."

It was so weird hearing him talk like this; I could tell it was weird for him too. He had this look of surprise on his face, like he couldn't believe the things he was saying.

"I just couldn't handle the idea that Hayden would succeed where I failed. And so I went to that party and told him that Athena wasn't real. I told him it was all a joke, that Astrid and I were in on it together, that she'd never really been his friend. He didn't want to believe me, but he couldn't argue when he saw Jess's text message." He looked down at the Smiths shirt. "I saw Mom packing up the box of stuff to give to you. It never occurred to her that I might want something to remember him by. This was the only band he listened to that I didn't hate, so I took it before she left."

I thought about some of the other songs on the playlist, like the one about siblings that I'd never fully understood. The lyrics were sad, but it was kind of a happy-sounding song. I wondered what Hayden had been trying to tell me about Ryan, whether he'd had any idea that the way Ryan treated him came from such a sad place. Maybe, on some level, he knew. I wasn't really sure what to say, though. I'd spent years thinking of only the bad things he'd done, with no regard for what it might have been like to be him. His life seemed so charmed, especially when compared to Hayden's; it was confusing to think that he had his secrets, just like everyone else.

"I know you blame me," he said. "And that's fair. I blame myself, too. And if you're the one who beat up Jason and Trevor, well, I guess I understand that, too."

"I didn't—" I started to say, but he held up his hand.

"Doesn't matter," he said. "We all did a lot of bad things, and it makes sense that bad things would happen to us. But losing Hayden—I have to live with the fact that I can never fix this. My friends hurt people, sure, but those people will heal, just like Jason and Trevor will. Hayden's not here to heal, though, so I don't think I ever will, either."

I'd never imagined getting to a place where I could ever feel bad for Ryan, but right now, I did. "I know what you mean," I said.

"I can't ask you to forgive me," he said. "I can't forgive myself, anyway, so what would be the point? But do you think, someday, it might be possible for you not to hate me so much?"

I thought about that for a minute, about the ever-growing list of people who felt responsible for Hayden's death. We were all right, but we were all wrong at the same time. And ultimately Hayden was the one who'd made the decision. He was the one who'd left us here, trying to figure it out, never able to say we were sorry, to make things right. I would never understand how hurt and confused and hopeless he must have felt, to decide it wasn't worth trying, and I wasn't mad at him anymore for doing it, but I never wanted to feel that way. And I never wanted to feel like I'd made someone else feel that way, either.

"I don't hate you," I told Ryan, and I mostly meant it. "I don't hate anybody."

"Thanks," he said, and I understood what people meant when they talked about weights lifting from them. "It means a lot."

"I haven't finished going through all the T-shirts your mom brought over," I said. "You can come by sometime, if you want. See if there are any more you'd want to take with you."

"I'll do that," he said.

I walked back over to Rachel and Jimmy. "Rachel told me that was your friend's brother," Jimmy said. "You okay?"

I nodded. "Okay enough," I said.

"Come on, little brother," Rachel said. "Time to go home."

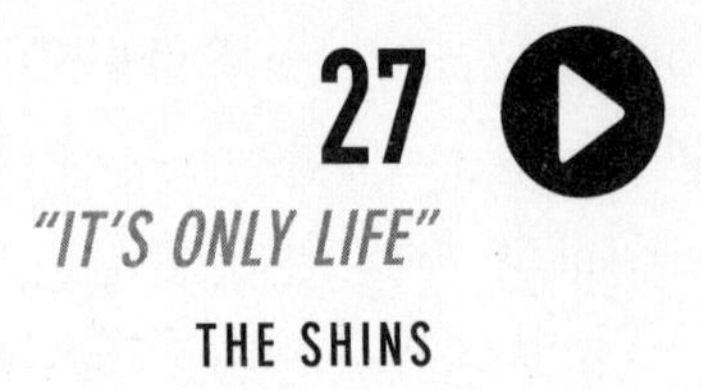

27

"IT'S ONLY LIFE"

THE SHINS

I WILL NEVER GET OVER THIS.

I know this to be true now, but I also know that not getting over it doesn't mean I won't someday be able to move on and live. Mr. Beaumont has helped me figure that out; I've been going to see him every week for the past year, and it's been a good thing. Mom was pushing for a real shrink for a while, but she's come to a couple of sessions with me, and I think she can tell that Mr. Beaumont is helping, so she's let it go. "For the time being," she says. I think she likes him; she gets kind of awkward around him in a way I'm not used to seeing her. I'm almost hoping that once I stop seeing him they might get together. It would be weird, but possibly also okay.

It's been a full year since Hayden died. I made it through the rest of sophomore year alone, burying myself in schoolwork, trying to get back into losing myself in books instead of in computer games, and though it was hard to concentrate for a long time, it got easier. I avoided Astrid and her friends, which wasn't all that hard; switching lunch periods made it easier, and I went back to my old habit of walking the halls looking down most of the time. It was different now, though—before I'd done it without thinking, because I didn't know another way. Now I was actively avoiding a life I knew might be out there. But it was my choice.

I visited my dad in California for the summer, which helped. He's still a d-bag, but he's my dad, and it was nice to get out of Libertyville. He lives near the water so I spent a lot of time at the beach, and I met some kids there who were pretty cool and welcoming, and it made me think that Hayden wasn't the only real friend I would ever have. There was even a girl I hung out with for a little while, though I never felt for her even a fraction of what I'd felt for Astrid.

The plan was to do the same thing junior year, to focus on academics and getting into a good school so I could get out of Libertyville and never come back. But loneliness is a thing that has weight, and it gets heavier over time, and it soon became clear to me that having friends for a summer was making it harder to function in a place where I had none.

I reached out to Damian first. Damian, the first one I'd been able to picture as my friend. I knew he'd been involved, but not with the worst of it. He told me it had started out as a prank; he hadn't realized how much things would escalate. He was still friends with them, but he'd pulled away a little, and we started hanging out. He wasn't Hayden, but he was a nice guy, and he was the one who was into graphic novels, so we got to talking about whether the movies based on Alan Moore books were any good. He showed me the stuff he'd been working on, and it turns out he's really talented. It's been nice having a friend again.

I've talked to Eric once in a while, too. I understand how mad he must have been about what happened to him, and even though I wish he'd done something to stop Astrid, I understood why he hadn't. I get that he was probably relieved that someone had decided to do something, even if it wasn't how he wanted it.

I still haven't figured out how I feel about Astrid. I know from Damian and Eric that she still wants to talk to me, and I know it doesn't make sense that I'd forgive them and not her. I just can't seem to wrap my head around the fact that she was responsible for the whole thing, that she felt like it was her job to avenge everyone's wrongs—Eric's, Jess's, hers, mine. Hayden's. There are days when I can almost grasp it, when I can feel understanding just ahead of me, and I can imagine forgiving the lies and the half-truths that kept me in the dark. Almost.

I know she catches me watching her every so often; she must be able to tell how hard it is for me not to run up to her every day and tell her I want to try again. And if she sees that, she must also see that in the battle between my impulses and all that lingering sadness and confusion over what it means to trust someone, even someone you haven't known very long, the confusion has won every time.

So far.

I ran into her in the cafeteria the other day; we still have the same lunch period sometimes. Often I'll see her across the room and she'll give me a little wave. Almost like a question that I'm never sure how to answer. That day, for the first time, I waved back.

My sister graduated last spring, and so did the bully trifecta. Rachel stuck with Jimmy until they both got into different colleges. He was my favorite of all the guys she ever dated; I'm hoping she gets back together with him someday. As for the bullies, Jason never came out, and he used his church scholarship to go to a little liberal arts college in Oregon. I'm sure he won't be back. Trevor healed surprisingly well, and he's at the state college, hoping to walk on to the hockey team. Ryan surprised me and didn't follow Trevor there; he went to a school back east, where I heard he wasn't playing football. I hoped it was because he'd chosen soccer. He never did come over to look at Hayden's shirts, but I hadn't really thought he would. They were all pretty quiet for the rest of the year, and word of all the things that had happened got out quickly, which seemed to make a difference. The lines between the social groups got pretty blurry; Eric started an LGBTQ/PFLAG group and more people joined than I would have thought. For most of the past year, Libertyville High has been at peace.

I'm hoping to get there myself someday. It took a while for me to feel comfortable using my computer again; I wasn't sure I wanted Archmage_Ged to come back. Eventually, though, I got back on; in talking to Mr. Beaumont I've come to realize that Archmage_Ged wasn't real. He was just something I made up to help me deal with everything. After all, he never really told me anything I didn't already know, whether I wanted to admit it or not. And given that getting regular sleep has made me feel like a different person, I have a better understanding of what not sleeping can do to someone. There had been something comforting about the idea that it was really Hayden, that he was still with me, creepy as it might be, but I think that was just something I needed for a little while. I've put the wizard figurine in a box for now, too. I'm glad I bought it, but I've stopped worrying about needing something to remind me of Hayden. He's here with me all the time.

These days I spend most of my time on the computer listening to music. I decided to retire Hayden's playlist. It never really solved the big mysteries for me, and I'll never be able to hear any of those songs again without going back to last year. But if it did anything for me, it was to actually get me to start talking to people. Or, rather, start listening to them. If there's one thing I learned from the playlist, it's how important listening to people can be. I like to think I'm getting better at it.

Hayden's playlist did make me feel connected to him, and it also opened me up to a lot of stuff I hadn't heard before, and I started looking for new bands, things I liked that I'd found on my own, not through Hayden or Rachel. I've even started making a new playlist myself, one more upbeat than the one Hayden sent me but maybe not as overly ecstatic as the ones he and Jess shared, one filled with songs that are bright and hopeful. Songs Astrid might like.

Maybe someday I'll give it to her.

ACKNOWLEDGMENTS

I have so many people to thank I barely know where to start.

Thanks to Melissa de la Cruz, Richard Abate, and everyone at Spilled Ink for taking a chance on me. Thanks to Jocelyn Davies and everyone at HarperCollins for their fantastic editing skills. Thanks to everyone at the Iowa Writers' Workshop, especially Frank Conroy (RIP), Sam Chang, Elizabeth McCracken, Connie Brothers, Deb West, and Jan Zenicek, for two of the best years of my life and more. Thanks to those who provided assistance and time, but especially Larry E. and Susannah B. Moore and the Corporation of Yaddo. Thanks to all the friends who provided help and advice and even housing, including but not limited to Katherine Bell, Justin Kramon, Elisa Lee, Dora Malech, Todd Pettys, Caroline Sheerin, Al Smith, Brandon Trissler, and Rebecca Trissler. Thanks to my fantastic writing group: Eugene Cross, Nami Mun, Samuel Park, Gus Rose, and Shauna Seliy. And finally, thanks to my family: Barry, Gail, David, and Marissa Falkoff, without whom nothing would be possible.